Each step she took led her closer...to terror

Marion slipped through the stillness of the woods, eager to see her friend Leon. Though it was late, she knew he'd be delighted to see her.

She looked up at his house, catching sight of a man's shadow framed in the window. "Leon!" she called softly. He turned around slowly, watching as she raced up the entrance steps.

But she stopped dead in her tracks when the door opened. It wasn't Leon.... She was staring into the eyes of a stranger, his expression oddly twisted. Suddenly she screamed, fighting the hands that now encircled her neck....

Other

MYSTIQUE BOOKS

by CLAUDETTE VIRMONNE

For a free catalogue listing all available Mystique Books,
send your name and address to:

MYSTIQUE BOOKS
M.P.O. Box 707, Niagara Falls, NY 14302
In Canada: 649 Ontario St., Stratford, Ontario N5A 6W2

To Court Danger

by CLAUDETTE VIRMONNE

MYSTIQUE BOOKS

TORONTO • LONDON • NEW YORK
HAMBURG • AMSTERDAM • STOCKHOLM

Chapter 1

"Are you tired, darling?" The man at the wheel of the sleek Jaguar took his eyes from the winding country road to glance briefly at his companion.

"Not at all," Marion replied with a smile, lifting her head and opening her gray eyes. Her fine dark brown hair fell in wisps of curls around her delicate oval face, giving her the look of a disheveled angel. "I was only dreaming for a moment. I was trying to imagine what its going to be like—your home, your mother. That's all."

"Stepmother," Jeremy corrected her.

"But you call her mother, don't you?"

"Yes, sometimes. But, to tell you the truth, I always think of her as my stepmother. I was twelve when she married my father."

"Did you find it difficult getting used to a new mother?"

"Not really," Jeremy answered, glancing at Marion. He pushed his blond hair back from his clear blue eyes. He shifted in his seat. The road was straight now, so, taking his gloved hand from the wheel, he took Marion's hand in his. "Are you worried that *you* might find it difficult?"

"Well, I can't help but worry," Marion confessed.

There were times when she felt like a princess in a beautiful though strange world. There also were times when she felt like an imposter, like someone who had no right to be where she was, to be the woman Jeremy Koster had chosen to give his name, his wealth, his love. So much had happened to her so fast. She had met Jeremy only three weeks ago, and now, here she was, Jeremy's fiancée, going to live with his family in their private château. In less than two weeks they would be man and wife.

In a hesitant voice that revealed her shyness and anxiety Marion said, "Jeremy, there's something I must ask you. Your stepmother is from a noble family."

"That's right. Her family goes back to the tenth century, when it was established by Siegfried, Count of Moselle. One of her ancestors, Ludovic, was aide-de-camp to Austria's Maximilian when he went to Mexico." He stopped, frowning, as if something unpleasant had suddenly occurred to him. "But I've told you all this."

"Yes. What I want to ask you.... Promise you won't get angry? Won't your stepmother be disappointed that you've chosen someone like me to be your wife? Wouldn't she rather see you marry someone wealthy, from an aristocratic family?"

"No, I promise you," Jeremy assured her, squeezing her hand. "My stepmother is going to like you. She's a very down-to-earth person."

"But Jeremy, be realistic," Marion pleaded, fearing that she was going to cry. She didn't know what had come over her. Perhaps it was the anxiety of the time growing so short. She was apprehensive. What if she didn't like their home? What if Jeremy's stepmother didn't like her?

"Marion, you're upset now. I'm sorry. What have I said? What have I done?"

"No, it's not you, Jeremy," Marion smiled, feeling foolishly young and unsophisticated. Jeremy was thirty-eight years old, and she was merely twenty-one. He was confident, successful, well educated, wealthy. She was young, inexperienced, poor and without family. *What can I offer him*, she often wondered. "It's . . ." she groped for words, "it's just that I keep wondering how she is going to react when she meets her future daughter-in-law: Marion Charles, sales clerk, orphan."

Jeremy turned to look at her. For a moment he examined her delicate profile. Her soft skin was the color of ivory, her hair was dark brown and silky and the large gray eyes, which sometimes seemed almost violet, were fringed by long dark eyelashes. But her most noticeable feature was her expression: the gentle curve of sensitive lips complemented by the eyes that were just barely touched with sadness.

With a smile of appreciation he turned his attention back to the road ahead. "Don't worry, Marion. She won't be disappointed, you can be sure of that. When I told her that I wanted to marry you, I also told her a little about you. She wasn't opposed to the idea at all. As a matter of fact, she seemed quite pleased." He paused before going on. "Martha, my stepmother, is quite open minded and free from prejudice. She married my father, and he was a commoner. He owned a small factory and had little money, and she was a very wealthy woman. She's going to love you, you'll see."

He gently caressed her delicate fingers. "There isn't a thing for you to be worried about. In a day or two my stepmother will be completely won over by your charm."

He smiled warmly at her. With his faultless profile and abundant ash-blond hair, Jeremy Koster was incredibly handsome. Although he was thirty-eight, seventeen years Marion's senior, his tanned face was that of a young man. His eyes were as clear and blue as a mountain lake and there was not the slightest sign of aging anywhere in his lean body.

Almost as if to tone down the impact of his splendid physique, he always dressed conservatively in suits of dark gray and blue and he wore plain silk ties in subtle colors. He was always solicitous of his fiancée and his manners were courtly and considerate.

Marion was enchanted with him. Jeremy had all of the qualities a young, romantic woman could wish for in her future husband, and she could scarcely believe that a man like Jeremy could be in love with her—he could have picked someone far more sophisticated. She often asked herself why he had chosen her. And then, one day, she asked him. "Why me? There are so many women in Paris...and elsewhere, for that matter. You could have fallen in love with any one of them."

His answer still rang in her ears. "Oh, I've known some beautiful women, Marion...even thought I was in love with one or two of them. But you're the only one I've ever wanted to marry." And with old-fashioned gallantry, he had bowed and kissed her hand.

The car rolled smoothly along the road, leaving behind the lush farmland and vast plains to enter a different kind of terrain. Now it was rugged with sweeping hills and deep valleys. It was springtime, and the delicate green of new buds mingled with the browns and rusts of old leaves and the darker green of the fir trees.

As the car moved ahead thoughts flashed through Marion's head as quickly as the trees alongside the road flashed past her eyes. She was thinking back to the time and place she had met Jeremy, the man she was going to marry, the fiancée who now was taking her home for their wedding. Was it possible that only three weeks had gone by?

SHE WOULD NEVER FORGET the day she met him. It was March, although the weather was much more like mid winter. Wet snow was falling and the sidewalks outside the exclusive fashion shop where she worked were very slippery.

It was late in the morning when Jeremy entered the shop. He was carrying a number of dresses that needed alteration. The women who worked in the shop—the models, and even the seamstresses—immediately took notice of him. Marion was standing behind the front counter, so she was able to hear everything he said.

Something about the way his eyes met hers had startled her, making her heart jump. His intense blue eyes were so determined that she felt she had been hit by some strong force.

Carmen, the manager of the shop, went to meet him. "Good morning, my name is Carmen," she introduced herself. "I am the manager." Rarely did they see a man come into the shop alone, and then it was usually to buy a gift for a wife or mistress. And rarely did a man who combined such obvious wealth and good looks come in. This had not been lost on Carmen, a woman who had no confusion about what she wanted in a man—except that she could never seem to restrict her needs to only one man. "Can I help you in any way?" Carmen went on, in what Marion recognized was her most seductive voice.

"Yes, please. I understand that this is the best place in Paris for high quality, custom fashion design."

"Of course, that is our reputation, and our clients agree."

"My stepmother, who is too ill to come into Paris—we live in the Vosges district—asked me to bring in these dresses. They are outdated, but perfectly good. She was wondering if you might be able to do something with them—make them more fashionable." He was standing so that he was facing Marion, and she had the uncomfortable feeling that his eyes never left her. Timidly she raised her eyes to look at him and was shocked by the ready and penetrating stare of his transparent blue eyes.

"Yes, Mr. . . . ?"

"Koster. Jeremy Koster. . . . Good," he added, as if he had forgotten himself for a moment. "May I leave them with you for a week? In the mean time, my stepmother is a size sixteen. Do you carry anything in that size?"

"No, I'm sorry we don't. Not at this moment."

"Well, a fourteen will do. I'll ask your sales clerk to show me what you have."

"I can show you, Mr. Koster," Carmen objected, but it was too late; Jeremy was already at Marion's side, subtly insisting that she be the one to help him.

Marion blushed and the women in the shop laughed to themselves and looked away. Afterward she had to put up with a lot of kidding about Jeremy, but their kidding grew to awe and amazement as his attentions became more ardent and extravagant over the next few days.

During that first meeting he admired her sweater, an attractive and original design that she had made herself. He explained that he owned a knitting mill, and that he would like to talk to her about her designs. He persuaded her so earnestly to join him for lunch that she couldn't refuse.

They had lunch at Julien's, a very expensive restaurant within walking distance of the shop. He urged her to order her heart's desire, and to drink at least some of the small bottle of vintage champagne that he had ordered for himself. Together they had talked and laughed. Marion's heart had soared with the attention and the wonderful things he told her. Their lunch had been long and leisurely—Carmen had told Marion, with a knowing wink, not to hurry back—and it wasn't over until Marion agreed to meet Jeremy for dinner that evening.

When she returned from lunch her friends at the shop crowded around her, wanting to know where they had gone, what Marion had eaten, how much it had cost, and, most especially, what he was like. Marion felt light-headed and giddy, a state she blamed on the champagne, but Carmen and the women in the shop laughed and told her otherwise. "It's love, Marion, that's what's wrong with you," they teased when she put a dress on the wrong rack for the fourth time that afternoon.

That evening, Jeremy picked Marion up at her rooming house. She was ready to go as soon as he got there—she hadn't wanted to keep him waiting in her shabby room. She had no family, and her meager salary as a sales clerk provided her with only a small income. She could afford little else.

She was thankful that Carmen had insisted on lending her a fashionable outfit for the evening. Otherwise she would have felt embarrassed to enter a good restaurant in her worn and simple clothes. When working, Carmen insisted that her employees change into beautiful clothes so that her customers, some of the richest and most aristocratic members of Parisian society, would feel that everything about the place was in the best of taste. Fortunately this meant that Marion didn't need to spend too much on a working wardrobe. It also meant that she had next to nothing appropriate to wear on an evening out.

Despite Marion's nervousness, Jeremy seemed totally unconcerned and relaxed. He ushered her to his gleaming black Jaguar, opening the door for her as if she were a princess. She slipped into the soft leather bucket seat, gathering her bright, flowered dress of fine lawn fabric around her. It was a beautiful evening and she felt light with happiness. Glancing at Jeremy, her heart leaped. Had she ever seen such a handsome man? She didn't think so. Everything about him was perfect.

Their dinner that evening set the stage for their evenings out every night of the weeks to come. With total ease Jeremy guided her through the crowded lines of the most exclusive restaurants in Paris. The maître d's invariably knew him well, welcoming him and guiding them to the best table in the house on a minute's notice. The waiters clustered around them. Would Mr. Koster like champagne? His favorite was in stock. How about the chef's special? It was cooked exactly to his taste that day.

Everywhere people knew Jeremy, important, newsworthy people—dignitaries, politicians, famous artists, heads of industry. They inevitably regarded Marion with a special curiosity and honored her with the most discreet respect. After all—she was with Jeremy Koster.

At first Marion felt ill at ease in this private, exclusive circle of the wealthiest and most successful people in France. How could she possibly belong? They were so well educated, so worldly—she could think of little to say to them. But Jeremy made sure she felt comfortable. His effusive compliments and continual gifts couldn't help but have an effect on her. She was loved by him and that was all that mattered.

After a week Marion even began to become accustomed to her new life in the heart of Parisian society. One very special evening they had lingered after dinner in an elegant, small dockside restaurant where the atmosphere was intimate and warm. Jeremy had asked for—and, of course, received—a special small room just for them. There at their own table, they had been able to enjoy the privacy and pleasure of each other's company, without the usual constant interruptions from the many important people Jeremy knew so well.

As they relaxed over coffee and liqueurs, Jeremy leaned toward Marion, who was seated kitty-corner from him, so that his handsome face was very close to hers. His voice was as soft as velvet. "Marion, will you marry me? Do you think you would like to be my wife?"

There had been times before when Marion had thought Jeremy was going to say those words, but it seemed just too fantastic to be anything more than her imagination. Now he had said them and she couldn't respond. She didn't know what to say. She could only gaze at him with a look charged with emotion. He reached his arm around her shoulder and pulled her to him, kissing her tenderly, passionately, urgently. "Marion, please, say yes," he whispered, his voice husky with desire. He kissed her again, holding his hand at the back of her neck, caressing the fine tendrils of her hair.

Marion's heart raced. She felt faint, weak with feeling. She longed to be gathered into his strong arms, to be cared for and caressed...to be loved. But she pulled herself away. The time had come. She had been both longing for and dreading this moment. "Jeremy, there are things I must tell you."

Now she had to tell him—things about herself, things that would make such a marriage impossible. With a trembling hand she stirred her coffee and hesitantly began to speak. "I was raised in an orphanage. I don't even know who I am. My name was created by some civil servant. I've lived in foster homes most of my life and I've been earning my own living since I was sixteen. Our worlds are completely different, Jeremy. You would soon regret marrying someone who could not fit into your kind of life." She sat up straight and, lifting her chin, looked steadily into his eyes. She spoke quietly. "I—I love you, but I love you too much to marry you."

She wiped the tears from her eyes. There was a moment of silence as she waited for his reaction. It would be all over for them now. Jeremy would disappear from her life; there would be no more magical evenings, no more the life of a fairy princess courted by a handsome prince. She would return to her drab and ordinary existence, her enchanting time with a man she loved a mere memory she would cherish for a lifetime.

"Marion, you can't refuse," Jeremy said simply. He seemed not at all shocked or surprised by what she had said—it was as if she were telling him something he had already known. "Don't you see," he went on, "I don't care about any of that. If you don't know who your parents are...what does that matter? Knowing that you've had an unhappy childhood only makes you that much more dear to me. It makes me want to make sure that you will be happy for the rest of your life. That is...if you'll let me. Marion, I love you. Please, you must say yes."

"Yes, Jeremy," Marion whispered, reaching for his hand, ignoring the tears that trickled down her suddenly glowing cheeks. "I love you, too, darling. I will marry you."

She turned away. The emotions she was feeling were too intense to bear—she would love him for the rest of her life.

Jeremy slipped his hand into his pocket and, with a triumphant grin on his face, brought forth a small blue velvet jewelry box and placed it in front of Marion. "Open it—it's for you," he said. Marion was trembling as she slowly lifted the lid of the beautiful box. Inside, nestled in pale blue satin was a ring, a simple gold band holding the largest diamond Marion had ever seen, its chiseled surface throwing a shower of light.

"Jeremy, you shouldn't—"

"Darling," Jeremy scolded her gently, slipped the ring on her finger and kissed her tenderly, "now that we're officially going to be married—soon I hope—you won't be able to turn my gifts away any longer. You might as well get used to the idea—I intend to give you everything you ever wanted...and more."

He took her into his arms again and kissed her ardently over and over again. Marion caught a glimpse of the exquisite ring on her finger. It *was* real—she and Jeremy were going to be married.

THE WOMEN Marion worked with could hardly believe that she was actually going to marry such a wealthy, handsome man. The back room fairly buzzed with chatter when there were no customers in the shop.

"Your fiancé is the best-looking man I've ever seen," declared Helen, the other sales clerk. "It should be against the law for a man to be that handsome. How did you manage to snare him?"

They all looked upon Marion with a touch of envy, wondering what she had that they didn't have.

"It must be those violet eyes and that ivory skin," said Patricia, a willowy blond model who was Marion's closest friend.

They all agreed that Marion was a very lucky young woman, all, that is except one....

"He's handsome, all right, I have to go along with that," said Ruth, who was very petite and as perfect as a porcelain doll. "But I don't like his eyes. They're as cold as ice."

Marion was offended, but she smiled and shook her head. *Ruth must be jealous*, she thought. Marion knew she was very fortunate. To her, it was like a fairy tale come true...and Jeremy was Prince Charming. Nevertheless she had her moments of doubt. Everything seemed almost too good to be true. A little voice deep inside kept telling her that there must be a catch, somewhere...but she refused to listen.

Shortly before they were due to leave for Grunberg, a strange dream began to disturb her nights. On a beautiful sunny day she would be dressed for the wedding, waiting for the guests to arrive. Everyone seemed very happy. And then the sky would darken and great clouds would suddenly come rushing across the sky. The faces of the guests would become gloomy and their clothing would change from colorful to somber, until the occasion seemed much more like a funeral than a wedding. Whispers would start, then grow to become shouts, "There'll be no wedding! There'll be no wedding!"

Every time she had this dream she would wake up exhausted, feeling depressed and apprehensive. She felt that Jeremy—so confident and certain of what he wanted—would laugh at her fears. So she didn't mention the dream to him.

Now she was heading toward Grunberg, the place where they would be married, where they would live. She was sure that there would be obstacles, and she suspected that one of them would be Mrs. Koster, who couldn't possibly be very happy about her son marrying someone with such an ordinary background. The gap between a family founded on generations of princely tradition and a woman whose family was unknown seemed enormous to her.

Chapter 2

It was the end of the day. The last traces of pale sunset could be seen on the red tiled roofs of the houses, the Swisslike chalets, the old farmhouses where rounded walls for the ancient bread ovens could still be seen. Slow-moving cattle grazed in the fields in their pastoral setting against the forest of evergreens. It was very peaceful.

Marion and Jeremy passed a long narrow lake. Then they entered a prosperous-looking town where people were busy dismantling the stalls after an all-day open market. Pointing to a group of buildings whose chimneys stood tall against the sky, Jeremy said that that was the mill. "Maybe I'll have a chance to show you around tomorrow." He took her hand in his. "By the way, my mother wrote that she's having a wing of the château renovated for us. It won't be ready for a while, of course, but I've already told her the name of the interior designer in Paris I want to work on it. He's the best—I know that he'll make our home a showpiece you'll be proud of."

Marion said nothing. She had hoped that they could pick things out together—just she and Jeremy—but she knew that many things would have to change for her now. She was going to have to get used to living in an entirely different way, she thought, snuggling into the soft white chinchilla sweater Jeremy had insisted on buying her.

It worried her, this amazing wealth that was taken so casually, so without thought or concern, but there was a part of her that loved it, too. Yes, she knew that there would be changes, and that some of these she wouldn't care for, but all in all she felt challenged and, despite her fears, quietly thrilled.

The scenery was gradually losing its color in the evening mist. The road they were traveling on through the trees was getting darker and darker.

"This is Ramberpont Forest we're in now. We'll soon be there."

"It has the feel of a forest where legends are born," Marion said.

"Legends are very plentiful in this area. Many originate in Alsace and are German. Marguerite, one of the old servants at the château, will be very happy to tell you as many as you want to hear."

The road, lined with tall evergreens, started up a sharp incline. Marion opened the car window to enjoy the scents of fresh grass, resin, and the sight of snow patches still visible here and there among the trees. From time to time she could hear the roar of water rushing down the slopes.

The car was climbing smoothly and swiftly when a man suddenly appeared on the road in front of them. "Brace yourself," Jeremy ordered, skillfully bringing the car to an abrupt halt.

The car stopped only inches from the shadowy motionless figure. He was a tall man, like Jeremy, but more muscular and darker. Wearing high boots and a rifle slung from his shoulder, he seemed like a pirate—a man whose bearing was so individual, so free, that he would always give the impression of standing alone, outside the crowd. Under the brim of his felt hat, his face expressed disdain. He stared boldly in the window and then, with a salute more insolent than friendly, he stepped aside to let the car go by.

"That's Leon Altamira, the manager of the estate," Jeremy growled. "At least mother calls him the manager. I call him the warden. I've never been able to understand how she can stand to have someone as arrogant as he is around."

With a frown he continued. "If it were up to me he'd have been gone long ago." His voice was harsh and his face flushed with anger. Marion couldn't accept the transformation. Jeremy had always been even tempered with her, never raising his voice. She was astonished at how quickly he had become upset, how violently he had spoken.

They continued in silence until the road widened into a clearing. And there it was...the château. It was magnificent. Solidly built of gray granite block, it stood proudly against the sky. Typical of many old castles, its architectural changes marked the succession of centuries. The lawn was manicured and the early spring flower beds were carefully tended. The colorful blooms glowed against the dark green background.

Seeing it for the first time, Marion was shaken. It was so much more grand, more beautiful, than she had imagined. To think that this was going to be her home...she couldn't believe it. She walked through the front door on Jeremy's arm, awestruck by the coats-of-arms and crests that covered the walls of the entrance, marveling at the high ceilings and vast proportions.

After giving a quiet order to the servant who had hurried to greet him, Jeremy took Marion into an adjoining room where a fire roared in a huge stone fireplace, above which was carved the family crest.

Two elderly women were seated in plush, plum-velvet wingback chairs beside the fireplace. One, who could only be described as plump, wore an exquisite dress hand-embroidered in shades of blue and gray. She seemed fragile, her delicate features and silvery hair discreetly revealing the signs of approaching age. Marion guessed that she was between sixty and seventy years old. Her gray eyes were very bright, and she had a quiet air of regal dignity. Marion hoped that she would be Martha Koster, Jeremy's stepmother.

The other woman, who appeared to be much the same age, was tall and quite thin. She had very large pale blue eyes and reddish hair. It was evident that she had been a beautiful woman when young; her features, like Jeremy's, were even and well proportioned. But she had lost much of her beauty with age, her once-handsome features now disguised by harsh lines and creases, carving a frowning and embittered expression into her face. Her chiseled lips were taut and drawn into a line of permanent disappointment and dissatisfaction. She rose to greet them, carefully arranging the folds of her obviously expensive green silk dressing gown around her. She extended a hand glittering with jewels.

Marion's heart sank. *Was this woman Jeremy's stepmother, her future mother-in-law?* With a sigh of relief, Marion felt Jeremy steering her toward the woman sitting in the chair.

"Mother, this is my fiancée, Marion," he said with a smile.

"Come closer," the woman urged.

Mrs. Koster suddenly smiled and Marion was captivated. She had been so apprehensive about this moment, afraid that Jeremy's stepmother might be less than pleased to meet her.

"Welcome to Grunberg, my child," she said gently, looking straight into Marion's eyes. "You will bring new life to these old gray walls. I hope you'll be very happy here." She held Marion's hand warmly.

"Thank you," said the young woman, deeply touched. "I'll try to be everything you may hope me to be."

There was a moment of silence. Marion and Martha looked at each other, openly and with a special charged emotion. For reasons she could not explain, Marion felt tears coming to her eyes.

"Marion," Jeremy said abruptly. "I would like you to meet my cousin, Isabel."

Marion was surprised that the other woman was Jeremy's cousin—she had never heard him mention her. She shook the hand extended to her. Isabel's words were for Jeremy. "I've had only two letters from you in the past month," she said petulantly. "You've written to Martha far more often than that."

"My dear," said Martha Koster. "I wish you'd stop thinking of Jeremy as your sole property. He's not a child anymore. He's thirty-eight years old and will be married soon. It's a time for happiness."

Martha Koster gestured to Marion and Jeremy and smiled warmly. "Do sit down, both of you. Did you have a good trip?"

"Excellent, thank you," Marion replied as she lowered herself onto a sofa with Jeremy. It was covered with linen striped in a rainbow of soft pastels. The abundant, plump cushions were down filled. A maid respectfully offered them a tray of canapés and quietly asked what type of drinks they would prefer. Marion sighed happily and squeezed Jeremy's hand.

"How do you like this part of the country?" Martha Koster asked after the maid had left.

"I think it's beautiful."

The mistress of the château nodded. "It is beautiful. You are seeing it for the first time in its most enchanting season . . . which, unfortunately, is also the shortest. It's spring, almost summer in fact, which doesn't last very long, either. Winter, of course, can be very harsh in these parts. It seems very peaceful here, but that is mostly on the surface. This is a land of burning passions, most of which have been kept hidden," she added with playful drama.

If there was a special meaning in her last sentence, no one seemed to pay any attention to it. The fire reflecting on the gleaming oak floor cast a warm glow on the furniture. The sun had set and an evening wind was rising, bringing with it the murmur of the forest, somewhat caressing, somewhat menacing.

"Yes," Jeremy's stepmother went on dreamily, momentarily interrupted by an eerie howl. "It's only the wind," she explained. "Soon the real wolves will start their howling."

Marion shivered, captivated by Martha's melodious voice and intrigued by the romance of her new home.

After a moment of silence Jeremy spoke up. "We met Leon on the road a little while ago. That man is becoming more and more obnoxious. He refused to move out of the path of the car, and then he barely acknowledged us. Really, I just can't see why you keep him around."

Mrs. Koster sighed, displaying a touch of annoyance. "You're wrong about Leon. We are very lucky to have him. He has an excellent education—a doctorate I believe—and could get a much better job if he wanted. I've heard that he is rather well known in the field of forestry as a matter of fact, and that he has published several books."

"Then why doesn't he get another job?" Jeremy asked, his voice bitter.

"I'm not sure why he continues to work for me. I guess he likes this part of the country and his hours—which aren't demanding. He has plenty of time for writing. And I've just recently told him that he could use the northeast hundred for testing—something to do with developing measures that would prevent damage from acid rain. I'm not sure exactly what. Frankly, I've never been able to understand why you two can't get along all of a sudden. I find him so interesting to talk to. Besides, I want him to stay. I have the highest regard for his services."

"Well—I simply don't like him," Jeremy said flatly. "And there are things you don't know about him that I'd rather not tell you," he muttered mysteriously under his breath. "Besides, I find his attitude unbearable and his pride totally inappropriate to his position. Why should he be so cocky?"

"Leon's personal life does not concern me, Jeremy. And you didn't always have this dislike for Leon. If I remember correctly there was a time when you were friends."

The color rose in Jeremy's face. Obviously ill at ease, he had to agree. "Yes, but lately his manners have started to annoy me."

Mrs. Koster looked at her stepson quizzically. "What happened between the two of you, anyway?"

Jeremy's face was now quite red. "Nothing...nothing at all."

"I've been around a little too long to believe that," Mrs. Koster said, shaking her head. "There must be something underneath all this."

She looked at Jeremy intently as he answered her quite irritably, "Now is not the time for this, mother. Besides, what could possibly have happened?"

"I'm sure I don't know. At any rate I don't suppose it's really any of my business. But I have to say that Leon has always been very considerate toward me and I have no reason to be dissatisfied with him. And I'll thank you to stop trying to impose your dislike for him on me."

It was than that Marion realized what a strong sense of justice and strength of will Martha Koster had—quite astonishing in a woman who appeared to be so frail.

Mrs. Koster continued in a much lighter tone, chuckling with good humor, "Anyway, you should know by now that I always have my way."

The conversation took a different direction and there was no further talk about the manager. Isabel, who had been silently sitting in her chair staring at the wall, almost as if she were in a trance, suddenly came to life and filled Jeremy in on all the details of her acting class's latest session.

From what Marion could gather this was a passing interest in Isabel's life, but one that everyone encouraged her to pursue. At one point, when Isabel was re-enacting a scene where everything went wrong, Marion was relieved to see Jeremy smiling and laughing along with the rest of them. Little by little he became calm and relaxed once more.

A short while later they went into the adjoining dining room, where an elegant dinner was served on a massively ornate table. The silver serving dishes reflected the dancing light from the log fire burning in a huge fireplace.

Marion found herself observing Isabel closely. Her attitudes and actions seemed full of contradictions and mixed emotions. At times she behaved like a lady-in-waiting, anticipating Martha Koster's every need. She would place a shawl around Mrs. Koster's shoulders, remind her of the pills that had to be taken and generally appear very solicitous, even though this attitude seemed to irritate Jeremy's stepmother at times. Marion wondered if it was bitterness that she saw in Isabel's eyes—or jealousy? She couldn't be sure.

On the other hand, when Isabel looked at Jeremy, the adoration in her eyes was unmistakable, an affection that Jeremy seemed to ignore. Toward Marion, Isabel was distant, but she was also adamantly enthusiastic about the coming wedding, and plagued Jeremy with questions about every detail.

Although Marion's feelings about Isabel were confused, she was greatly relieved and almost jubilant about Martha, Jeremy's stepmother, whom she was finding to be such a delightful—and even lovable—person. Throughout dinner Marion was kept smiling and laughing over Martha Koster's stories and amusing observations on life. She felt that she could listen to her for hours on end and still want to hear more. She was such a confident woman, so...regal was the only word that Marion felt really suited her. She could be firm and commanding one minute, as she had on the matter of Leon Altamira, and warm, gracious, and entertaining the next.

Dinner was served in several courses, each dish more outstanding than the last. Their Parisian chef had been hard to find, Isabel informed her, but he was doing the job "adequately."

"But this food is superb," Marion protested.

"Of course it is, dear," Martha said with a smile. "Soon you will be used to us all. Isabel always complains; I always praise; and Jeremy always orders us around. We are a typical family."

Marion smiled and caught Jeremy's eye. His handsome features were even more attractive in the flickering light of the crystal candelabra. He gave her a knowing smile back. She had felt like an outsider all of her life. Now she would be part of a "real" family—and she felt she was going to like it.

"I'M SO HAPPY, SWEETHEART," she whispered to Jeremy later, after a relaxing evening's talk around the fireplace. Jeremy was leading her up the grand oak staircase to her room on the second floor. "I really like your stepmother."

"I'm glad. I knew you would," Jeremy smiled, putting his arm around her slender waist and giving her an affectionate squeeze.

Marion felt very small and delicate next to Jeremy, who was so muscular and aggressive in his movements. He was a man of the world, and it showed in his air of confidence. Marion loved being with him; she loved the security, knowing that everything would be taken care of, that there was nothing for her to worry about—ever. After a lifetime of looking after herself, being the fiancée of a man like Jeremy was an incredible pleasure. At first she had tried to resist. The gifts, the lavish evenings out, and the first-class accommodations had overwhelmed her, making her feel uncomfortable and insecure at times. But Jeremy had convinced her that it was important to him—that he loved her with all his heart, and that he wanted to share everything with her, especially his abundant wealth.

At the top of the stairs Jeremy guided her to the right. "Mother said that she has had the Jasmine Room prepared for you. I think you will like it. It's a little old-fashioned, but it's comfortable and light."

He opened a mahogany door with a gleaming brass doorknob onto a large airy room. A fire in a corner fireplace with a simple, carved wooden mantel threw rosy light over the room. Jeremy flicked on the light switch, and a number of soft, small lamps placed discreetly around the room burst into light, creating a warm, welcoming atmosphere. A large four-poster stood against one wall, supporting a canopy of what appeared to be white ruffled organdy. The curtains that enclosed the bed had been drawn open to reveal an inviting interior complete with a soft down comforter and a heap of feather pillows. A homespun wool braided rug, simple wooden antique furniture—a rocker, a desk—and a cheerful love seat and armchair upholstered in what seemed to be an old-fashioned quilt, gave the room a charming, tasteful look.

"Oh, Jeremy," Marion sighed. "I love it. I've never seen a room so beautiful."

"This room? It's okay I suppose," Jeremy said casually as he strode across the room and threw open two French doors Marion hadn't noticed at the far end of the room. "Come—it's not too cold. Take a look outside."

"How nice," Marion exclaimed. "What a wonderful spot to sunbathe and read."

"Umm, yes," Jeremy agreed, gathering her into his arms more tenderly than usual. "Good night, my dearest, my princess," he murmured passionately. He tilted her lips to his and kissed her long and deeply, leaving Marion's heart racing, and her body faint with desire.

"Sleep well," he whispered in her ear, softly kissing her shoulders and neck. "Sleep well under this roof—it will soon be yours."

He held her for a moment in his arms, close against his chest.

"My love," Marion murmured, almost to herself. Was it true?

Was this happiness real? Was it hers? Her head was spinning as he turned to leave.

For a while Marion stood against the balcony railing, looking out over the forest, listening to the rich night sounds. *I am going to learn what each of those sounds are,* she vowed. *I am going to learn about each tree, every flower. I am going to know this land better than I have ever known anything.*

It was chilly. Reluctantly she went back into the room and closed the doors behind her. She was tired. She would take a long hot bath and curl up for the night. The door to the right was slightly ajar and she guessed that it was the bathroom. She pushed the door open . The room was larger than any bathroom she had ever seen. It had a huge, old-fashioned marble bathtub with crystal taps. A pink pedestal basin shaped like a delicate shell stood in one corner. Rich, fleecy towels were draped over a white wicker stool, together with a parcel, wrapped in shiny geometric paper and gold ribbon.

A present? For me, Marion wondered. Hesitantly she picked up the parcel and found a card. "For my future wife on her first night in her new home. Love, Jeremy."

Marion shook her head fondly. Jeremy could be so romantic sometimes. Eagerly she opened the parcel. Inside she found a thick, velvet robe in a pearl gray that suited her perfectly. Inside were tucked matching slippers and another parcel. "For my future wife on her first night in her new bed. Love, Jeremy," the note said. Again Marion unwrapped the gleaming paper. This time she found a long, pale lilac nightgown of fine embroidered silk. The design was simple, with an understated elegance that Marion loved.

"Oh, it's beautiful," she sighed, and held it up in front of a full-length mirror framed in white wicker. "Thank you, my love," she said wistfully, hugging the gown to her.

Eagerly she ran her bath, scenting it from the assortment of oils and herbs set out on the marble shelf at one end of the bath. After a long soak she slipped into her gown, and feeling every inch a pampered princess, she turned off the lights and climbed into her soft bed, pulling the silk sheets and cozy down comforter around her. From time to time there seemed to be the murmur of soft voices, as though something remained of those who had lived and loved in this ancestral home. As she listened to the whispers of the night Marion lay quietly, thinking that it would be here, in this castle, that she would be spending the rest of her life. A page had turned and a new chapter in her life was about to begin.

Dreamily, soothed by the luxurious feel of her fine silk gown and sheets, Marion drifted into sleep, only to be startled, momentarily, by the painful memory of a haunting dream—a dream that broke her peace night after night, a dream of humiliation...and terrible loss.

Chapter 3

Exhausted from the trip, Marion slept soundly, awakening the next morning only when she felt a slight nudge at her feet. She opened her eyes to see a beautiful striped cat at the foot of her bed, fixing her with the stare of golden enigmatic eyes. "Who are you?" she said aloud. "And how did you get in here?"

She looked around her room, feeling as if she had awakened in a strange and foreign land. A flood of sunlight poured in through the French doors and leaded windows, cheering her. Gradually it all came back. She felt the silken smoothness of her delicate lilac gown and smiled. Then she noticed that the door to her room was slightly open. Probably she hadn't shut it tight the night before. The cat moved closer, encouraged by Marion's friendly attitude. Purring, he continued to investigate various spots on the comforter before deciding on just the right one to curl up in and go to sleep. Amused, Marion moved over to give him more room.

A spring breeze rustled the curtains. Glancing at the tiny jeweled clock, Marion was surprised to see that it was already ten o'clock. Just as she was about to slip out of bed, there was a light knock at the door.

"Come in," she called.

In the doorway stood a small, wizened woman, wearing a black apron and a long, black cotton dress. "Excuse me, Miss Charles," she said in a hesitant voice. "I'm sorry to disturb you. I'm looking for my cat, Tiger...."

She stopped. "There you are, you bad cat! I should have known! You're very naughty!"

Hearing the familiar voice, the cat opened his eyes, but only momentarily. He immediately closed them again and settled himself to go back to sleep.

"He belongs to me," the old woman went on.

Judging by her attire Marion guessed that this woman was a servant, and yet she was bold and familiar in a friendly way.

"He has his own cushion and he had to choose yours. It must be the comforter on your bed that pleased him. Chase him off, if he's bothering you."

"But he isn't bothering me at all," Marion assured her. "I love cats...and this one is particularly beautiful."

The little woman straightened up and beamed with pleasure, like a mother whose child has received a compliment. "Just the same he's being very cheeky," she said. "If he starts to bother you, just chase him out of the room."

"Don't worry, I will," Marion smiled.

The woman turned to leave, then changed her mind. "Would you like to have your breakfast now?"

"Breakfast? Well, yes if it wouldn't be any trouble," Marion replied.

"No trouble at all. I'll send Jeanne up with it. What would you like? We have freshly baked croissants or rolls, fruit, cereal, eggs, bacon, ham or sausage, home fries. Even French toast or pancakes if you prefer. And, of course, we'll bring you hot coffee."

"I'll have croissants and fruit, thank you. And coffee." Marion smiled. It looked like she was just going to have to get used to being spoiled.

After a final try to convince the cat to go along with her, the woman gave up and left the room. A few moments later a young maid came in with a tray bearing a steaming pot of coffee, foaming milk, fresh, fragrant croissants and a basket containing an assortment of ripe fruit.

"Miss Charles, would you like to eat your breakfast at the table by the window or in bed? Or, since it's quite warm out, how would you like to eat on the balcony?"

"Oh, what a lovely idea. The balcony by all means," Marion exclaimed, slipping her toes over the edge of the bed and stretching contentedly. The bed was so high her feet didn't even reach the floor.

Tiger even perked up, and showing great interest in the food the maid was carrying, he followed her through the French door. Marion slipped into her new robe and slippers and went out onto the balcony. The day was crystal clear and bright. Marion was astonished that she could see for miles around, the heavily forested hills showing the occasional patch of snow in spite of the warm day. From not too far away Marion could make out a small clearing where a single wisp of smoke rose, as if from a fireplace. Down in the valley she could see the houses of the town and the chimneys of Jeremy's factory. Marion settled into one of the wicker chairs and was immediately pestered by Tiger, who was purring, mewing and rubbing himself against her legs insistently. Marion laughed and poured a little milk into a saucer and gave it to the cat.

"Talk about being spoiled!" exclaimed the young maid.

Because they were about the same age Marion felt less shy with this young woman and was comfortable enough to ask a few questions. "Whose cat is this, Jeanne?"

"He belongs to Marguerite, the old housekeeper."

"Is she the one who's supposed to know all the legends of the forest?"

The young girl smiled. "That's for sure. She knows everything there is to know about this area...and she loves to tell stories. I think she even makes up a few of her own."

She bent down to pick up the empty saucer while the

cat proceeded with the very serious business of washing himself.

"Marguerite has worked for Mrs. Koster for a very long time...more than forty years, I think. Now she's too old to do much in the way of actual work, but the mistress still keeps her on for mending and such. She lives in the servants' wing of the château, but her cat roams all over the place. She spends most of her time either looking for him or arguing with Beth, another woman almost as old as she is. I guess when people get to be their age, they have to find their fun whenever they can."

With these words, which said a good deal about the state of Marguerite's mind as well as her situation in the château, the maid left. The cat jumped onto the hammock and curled up for a nap.

After enjoying a relaxing breakfast in the sun Marion decided it was time to go downstairs. She wondered if Jeremy was up yet and what he had in mind for their first day here. While washing, she worried about what she was going to wear. She had many new outfits being made for her in Paris, but she wouldn't be getting those for at least a few days. Until then she had the clothes she had worn before she had met Jeremy, clothes that suddenly looked ragged and poor in this setting. True she had many of the luxurious items Jeremy had showered her with, but none of these seemed practical for today. The slacks and chinchilla sweater she had worn yesterday would have been perfect, only she recoiled from the idea of wearing the same outfit two days in a row, especially when she had just met these people. Finally after many changes of mind, she settled on a simple blue jersey dress that suited her well.

That decided, she dressed quickly and went downstairs to the living room where she found Martha Koster, looking somewhat different this morning because she was wearing glasses and reading a newspaper. At her side was Isabel, knitting a sweater. Martha greeted Marion with a warm smile.

"Did you sleep well?" she asked.

Marion was so in awe of Jeremy's stepmother that she had to stop herself from dropping a curtsy, as she had been taught to do at the orphanage. She then turned to greet Isabel, who also smiled at her.

After a few moments she asked where Jeremy was.

Martha smiled. "My dear, he left for the mill a long time ago. Despite his appearance as a romantic young man, he works very hard. He said that there were a number of things that needed to be straightened out at the mill and he couldn't do very much about them while he was in Paris."

"Yes, I understand," Marion murmured. Nevertheless she felt a stab of disappointment. After a moment she looked up, her expression anxious. "He'll be coming home for lunch, won't he?"

Martha shook her head. "I don't expect so. Usually he eats in the village or at the factory. That way he doesn't lose much time."

She paused before asking if Marion were disappointed.

"Yes, a little," Marion sighed. With Jeremy away she felt lost, like a stranger in this great château.

With a sort of mischievous kindness, the mistress of the château continued. "I guess you'll find time dragging a good deal while you wait for him to get home tonight, won't you, my dear?"

The young woman nodded and smiled shyly.

Mrs. Koster went on. "Well, I haven't forgotten what it's like to be young and in love. When you're waiting, a day seems like a hundred years. Now here's what I have in mind. I have a doctor's appointment at four, but I thought I would do some shopping beforehand. Why don't you come with me? Maybe we can even stop in at the mill. You can stay there or come along with me to the doctor. I'll leave it up to you."

"May I go with you, too, Martha? I want to see Jeremy," Isabel interrupted.

"That won't be necessary," Martha replied, her voice revealing a hint of irritation.

Isabel lowered her head, but not quickly enough to conceal the glint of spite in her eyes. Then she spoke "Well, anyway, I have to tell the seamstress what to do. I'd almost forgotten."

Satisfied at having found something she had to do, and thus saving face, Isabel left the room. When she had gone Mrs. Koster sighed.

"Oh, dear. I shouldn't have been so sharp with her, I suppose." Martha Koster glanced at Marion with a worried look in her eye. "It's just that. . . how can I put it? Isabel can be very demanding in her own way at times. I know she tries to be helpful, but somehow she often ends up being a bother. Well, I shouldn't be saying these things to you in any case. I only hope that you don't think poorly of us."

Marion smiled warmly, touched that this woman was willing to open up to her a little—to share her feelings and thoughts.

"I don't know if Jeremy has mentioned this," Martha went on, "but. . . you see, I was married twice. I had a very solid affection for my first husband, but I truly loved Jeremy's father. Life has brought me more than my share of grief, but the years I spent with him were some of the happiest I have known. When he died I was lost."

On the same sad note, she continued. "On his deathbed he left Jeremy and Isabel in my care. Isabel has never been. . . *well*, you see. There were times when she had to spend time in a hospital. And she was in very bad shape then. There was no choice but for me to look after her—even though we haven't always gotten along. And she loved Jeremy so, I couldn't separate them. She has been more of a mother to him than I have. Indeed, before I married Jeremy's father, Isabel was looking after the boy."

She shook her head. "I promised that I would look after her—and I have. Sometimes though, I can't hide my irritation and I hate myself for it because I know that Isabel is very devoted to me."

Recalling the expressions she had glimpsed in Isabel's eyes, Marion couldn't help but think that Mrs. Koster might do well to have some reservations about just how genuine Isabel's feelings actually were. Of course, she kept her thoughts to herself.

During lunch Isabel demonstrated the same eagerness to serve Mrs. Koster. When the meal was over Marion accompanied the mistress of the château to her car that the chauffeur had brought around to the front door. He drove the elegant Mercedes slowly and carefully, taking the same road that had brought Marion to the château.

At the first turn in the road Martha pointed out a narrow path into the woods.

"That path goes right to the factory, Marion. I know it well. In the days when Jeremy's father and I were courting, we used to meet and walk along that path constantly. It's a beautiful walk. It's been many years, but I remember every turn of it as if it were yesterday."

Martha sat back in the comfortable leather-upholstered seat, a tender smile on her lips and a far-away gaze in her eyes. Marion felt a rush of warmth for this aging woman. Martha had loved intensely, that she guessed, and that love was still, so many years later, an important part of her life.

Marion took the opportunity to admire the forest, where a light breeze stirred the leaves. The fir trees stood very tall, appearing to spread their great branches in a protective manner over the smaller trees and bushes and the delicate ferns. From time to time a squirrel could be seen leaping from branch to branch.

The road widened as they drove out of the forest into bright sunlight. Peaceful homes bordered the country road against a breathtaking backdrop of mountains and lake. In a field of wild flowers a donkey grazed, seemingly full of fairytale wisdom and that special hidden knowledge. It was a magical day.

They turned onto a special side road that led into the center of town. It seemed brighter and more elegant than it had the evening before when Marion and Jeremy had driven through at the day's end. In the late afternoon sun she could see the smartly yet casually dressed women of the area, noted for its fashionable and wealthy families, its charming and chic shops and variety of excellent entertainment from all parts of the world.

"It's a small town," Martha commented, holding onto Marion's arm as they walked down the cobblestone sidewalk. "And an ancient one, but I think you will find nothing lacking. Perhaps you will even come to love it as I do."

"I'm sure I will," Marion said, gazing around her with a sense of enchantment. The historic buildings fairly shone in the brilliant light. The narrow cobblestone streets glistened, and gay spring flowers were blossoming in boxes under each window. The town reflected the pride its inhabitants felt—not one detail had been overlooked. Everything was brightly painted and scrubbed.

"It's so different from Paris," Marion went on. "So clean...and fresh." She touched the gentle hand on her arm. "I think I love it already."

Martha smiled up at her. "Come," she said. "There's something I want to show you...and someone I want you to meet."

The little woman guided Marion through the streets to a small boutique off what appeared to be the central square.

They entered the shop, its simple antique facade belying the understated regal elegance inside. Marion caught her breath. The light filtered through the stained-glass windows onto a cascade of potted ferns beside a luxurious Prussian blue-velvet sofa and wingback chairs.

With a familiarity that told Marion that she came here often, Martha collapsed with a sign of obvious relief into the cushions.

"Come, my child. Sit down," she said, gesturing toward the chair opposite.

In a moment an exquisitely dressed woman of extraordinary appearance entered, followed by a young woman carrying a tray with steaming hot coffee and milk and an assortment of fresh fragrant pastries.

"You must be Marion," the woman said, graciously

extending her hand. "I'm Julia Martineau. Please call me Julia."

There are certain women who refuse to accept the fact that they are growing older and this woman was one of them. While Martha Koster used makeup discreetly and added a delicate tint to her hair, which was very becoming, her overall appearance remained very much in keeping with her age and dignity. Julia Martineau on the other hand, had dyed her hair a brilliant shade of blond, which defied any suggestion that it might be natural, and had made up her face as if she believed that quantity alone could hide her years. Mrs. Koster must surely have disapproved, and yet, she treated her friend with indulgence. It was instantly clear to Marion that the feeling that existed between these two women was of a deep and affectionate nature.

Mrs. Koster turned to look at Marion and made the introductions. "Marion, Julia and I have been friends since we were children," then added teasingly, "Julia, my dear, what do you think of Jeremy's fiancée?"

Mrs. Martineau blatantly stared at Marion, examining the lovely features and smiling to reveal what appeared to be an incredible number of false teeth.

"What a charming young woman," she cried effusively, nodding with such vigor that her hair bounced around. "Absolutely ravishing, darling! I must compliment you, my dear friend."

With a jerk of her head she turned to Martha Koster. "It's so nice to be young and in love," she continued. "It reminds me of my younger days... and yours, Martha." She heaved a great sigh. "That was many years ago... far too many to count! You know what I was thinking of the other day? I was remembering when I was eighteen, and madly in love with your cousin... the beautiful Leopold."

Mrs. Koster also sighed, and her eyes seemed to be looking into the distance.

"Yes, I remember." She turned to Marion: "Poor Leopold was killed in a plane crash during one of his many trips around the world in search of art objects. He was the last of the Sayn family and he died without an heir. With the exception of myself, there is no one with Sayn blood in their veins. Many of the men in that family died as warriors. They loved to go into battle and fight for causes they considered to be just and noble."

"Leopold was such a handsome young man, wasn't he?" declared Mrs. Martineau. "So tall, so virile, there was something positively regal about him. I was absolutely insane about him. Do you know, there's someone who reminds me very much of Leopold."

"Really? I can't imagine who it might be," Mrs. Koster said, obviously very much intrigued.

"Your manager, my dear. When I saw him last week when I came for tea, I knew he reminded me of someone, but I had a terrible time remembering who, and *now* I know. His mannerisms are very much like Leopold's. He has the same walk, and the same marvelous shade of dark red hair."

"You know, you may be right, Julia," Mrs. Koster finally agreed. "Now that you mention it, I realize that Leon does bear a resemblance to Leopold."

Marion was amused but only half-listening to what was being said. She couldn't imagine anyone looking like Leon Altamira. He was too much of an individual to be like anyone else. She sighed and forced herself to pay attention to the conversation. The talk turned from one thing to another, including a discussion of birthmarks, which often repeat themselves in different generations of the same family. And then the conversation turned to the wedding.

"Do you know, my dear young woman," said Mrs. Martineau, "that we thought for a while that Jeremy was never going to get married. It's quite an achievement for you to have changed his mind."

"Oh, but it turned out to be well worth the wait, didn't it," Martha Koster said warmly, making Marion blush.

They all turned when a woman came into the shop.

"Well, we should be going, Julia," she went on, rising

to her feet. May I use your phone to contact Henry?"

"Of course," Mrs. Martineau responded before greeting her customer. "I'll see you for lunch next Wednesday."

The two friends nodded an affectionate farewell and Martha and Marion went on their way.

"Well, I'm afraid we didn't do much shopping," Martha Koster laughed as they climbed into the car that Henry had drawn up to the front door. "That always happens to me when I visit Julia. I'm afraid that we get carried away. I think it's time we dropped in on Jeremy, don't you?"

Marion nodded happily as the car pulled away from the curb.

Gradually the chimneys of the factory came into view, their stacks towering over the landscape. The car slowed and then came to a stop in front of a building detached from the others. These were the offices.

Briskly for a woman of her age, Martha Koster led Marion through the labyrinth of halls and offices to the executive suites. Everywhere they turned employees greeted her with a smile and a courteous nod. Marion they regarded with open curiosity.

They crossed a small waiting room with several chairs and doors to reach Jeremy's office. Familiar with the place, Mrs. Koster headed straight for the door that opened into a large, bright room containing a desk, filing cabinets and a few other furnishings, all quite austere. Confidently, Martha knocked on Jeremy's office door and walked in, followed by Marion. Abruptly, they both stopped. A tall, stunningly beautiful woman jumped to her feet. Jeremy, who was standing behind his large, imposing desk, started to say something but apparently thought better of it.

The woman was about Marion's age, or slightly older. Blond with exquisitely molded features, she must have made many a man turn his head, Marion thought to herself. She was wearing a red jersey dress, its design surprisingly elegant, and clutched a handkerchief in one hand. Surprised, she stared at the two women and pressed the handkerchief to her lips. Her eyes were red and her cheeks wet. Marion knew at once that she had been crying. She seemed to hesitate for a moment, throwing a desperate look toward Marion, then turned and ran out the door.

"Who was that?" asked Marion.

"Her name is Ida Somers, isn't it, Jeremy?" replied Martha Koster. "She works here at the mill."

"This is an unexpected visit," Jeremy said. "Why didn't you call?"

"Because we wanted to surprise you," Martha Koster said. "What was that young woman crying about Jeremy? And why did she run out like that?"

Jeremy shook his head and waved his hand in an expression of disgust. "Oh, I don't really know for sure. She's been very upset lately, the girls tell me, and today she began acting strangely and crying. Man troubles they say. I called her in here to see if there was anything I could do to help...and that's when you came in. Really, mother, I would prefer it if you at least waited for me to ask you in. And where was Lilian?"

Martha shrugged her shoulders to show what she didn't know.

"I'm sorry, Jeremy. You're right, that was very rude of me. I guess I got carried away, remembering the old days. It's nice to see some familiar faces still around here. Older, but familiar nevertheless."

"Well, now that you're here, sit down." Jeremy gestured them toward two chairs. He eased himself into the large, well-worn leather chair behind his desk. He looked very attractive in his well-tailored suit, exuding an aura of power and confidence.

"And how are you, darling?" he asked, addressing Marion especially. "How has your day gone?"

"Very nicely. And thank you for your gifts last night, Jeremy."

"You liked them? I'm glad," he said, smiling warmly at her.

"I must go, Jeremy," Martha Koster said abruptly,

sensing their need to be alone. "I have a doctor's appointment downtown. I thought Marion could either stay here or accompany me."

"I'd love to have you stay here with me, darling, but I'm just too busy to be able to spend any time with you at all," Jeremy explained apologetically.

"Then come to the doctor's with me, Marion."

But the thought of staying indoors on such a beautiful sunny day didn't appeal to Marion. "If you don't mind, I think I'd rather just walk around and get to know the area a little. I'd like to walk back to the château. Couldn't I take that path you pointed out to me Martha?"

"Of course, but it's quite a walk," Mrs. Koster said.

"I don't mind. I've always enjoyed hiking."

Mrs. Koster sighed. "When I was young I used to love walking through the forest. Now I'm reduced to getting around by car. Of course I should be thankful that I have such a comfortable car to get around in. A rather melancholy advantage of old age, so to speak."

Looking out the window with a wistful smile, she went on. "A beautiful day like this is a blessing and you're quite right to want to take advantage of it. The path is about four miles. Is that too much for you?"

"Not at all," Marion replied with a smile. "I've walked farther than that in the streets of Paris, where it isn't nearly as healthy as walking here."

Mrs. Koster looked at the young girl warmly. "I think you're going to be a true mountain girl," she said, "and that pleases me very much."

Marion blushed with pleasure. Any sign of approval from Martha Koster was very important to her.

"Jeremy will show you where the path begins, I'm running a bit late. . . . I must be off. I'll see you both later."

She waved her hand as she went out the door, leaving the young couple on their own.

There was a moment of silence between them.

"Jeremy, that woman—Ida I think your mother said— seemed so desperate. Isn't there anything anyone can do?"

There was an element of nervousness in Jeremy's voice and his gestures seemed somewhat erratic instead of calm and measured as they normally were.

"Don't take Ida Somers too seriously, Marion. She is one of those people who needs a good talking to once in a while to keep her work performance at a high level," he continued with an annoyed frown. "If it isn't one thing with her it's another."

"I just don't like to see people so unhappy," Marion murmured.

In a tone that revealed a touch of impatience, Jeremy replied that sometimes it couldn't be avoided. Then in a softer voice he added, "Believe me, Marion, Ida isn't as upset as she seems. You'll just have to take my word for it."

She lifted her eyes and looked at him with tenderness. She had every confidence in him. Hadn't she put her own lifelong happiness into his hands? She was angry with herself for questioning things and meddling in matters that really didn't concern her. Wasn't it enough to be happy...to feel loved?

Jeremy leaned toward her and spoke in his most caressing and melodious voice. "You are an exquisite woman, Marion. And I love you all the more for being so sensitive...." His smile, his voice, his arms imprisoned her. Without concern for where they were, they exchanged a long ardent kiss. Marion's heart was filled with love and she felt happier than she had ever felt before in her life.

Chapter 4

The sharp ring of the telephone jolted Marion from her reverie. Smoothly, Jeremy reached over his massive mahogany desk to answer it.

"Koster here," he replied in a brisk businesslike manner, but the faint, shrill sound of a woman's voice and Jeremy's suddenly expressionless face told Marion that something was strangely wrong. "I'm sorry, you must have the wrong number," he said coldly and hung up. "Let's go, Marion," he announced abruptly. "I've got work to do."

Jeremy took Marion by the elbow and led her out of the office. As they left the executive offices, Jeremy turned to his secretary. "Lilian, you shouldn't have put that woman's call through," he said gruffly.

Lilian, a slender young woman who seemed very efficient, turned pale. "I'm sorry, I-I-I didn't—"

But she wasn't given a chance to finish. "Don't let it happen again." Jeremy turned and slammed the door behind them.

Marion was silent. She was afraid to say anything. Jeremy was obviously seething with anger and she feared she might be his next target if she said what was on her mind.

Frankly, his reactions upset her. *Why was he so angry over a wrong number? If it was a wrong number, why would he expect the woman to call him again?*

Within minutes they were outside the factory and the bracing spring air, with a hint of blooming flowers, refreshed her, bringing her back to the beautiful world around her.

"Why don't you walk back with me," she ventured gently. "It might be a good idea to take the afternoon off." She didn't know why he was so upset. Except for the day before, when he had been angry at the manager on the road, she had always known him to be cheerful and charming. She didn't feel that she could ask what was bothering him, yet she felt that she had to do something to help him, whatever his problem might be.

"Too much to do, Marion," Jeremy said, shaking his head, stopping at a place not far from the factory, at the edge of the woods.

"But, after all," Marion decided to press on, "we've only just got back. Couldn't you—?"

"No," Jeremy interrupted her sharply. "But I appreciate the thought," he added with a conscious effort to soften his manner. "You are a wonderful girl, Marion. You will make a very good wife."

Looking around to make sure no one could see them, Jeremy put his arms around her, pulling her slender body to him, and kissed her.

Marion surrendered herself to her fiancé's embrace, glad in her heart that whatever it was that was bothering him was passing, and that he was returning to his normal self, the man she loved and was going to marry. But his touch didn't move her and she was secretly relieved when he pulled away from her. It was as if his mind were elsewhere, although he was pretending that it wasn't so.

Why can't he confide in me, tell me what is bothering him, Marion wondered, but she guessed that that would come with time, and that they would become closer after they married.

Jeremy gave her directions, saying, "It's a long walk, but very pretty and not too steep," then kissed her again and turned back to the factory.

Marion stepped into the woods and turned to watch him make his way back, a surge of affection welling up inside her. Even now, now that they were going to be married, she found herself amazed by Jeremy. He was so handsome, so successful, so cultured, sophisticated and charming. Wherever they had gone in Paris women had warmed to him. It had been obvious to her that he could have had his pick. And yet he had chosen her—to love, to marry. Marion shook her head and smiled. It was almost too good to be true. After her lonely life, it was as if she had suddenly landed in the middle of a dreamworld. Sometimes she felt like pinching herself to see if she weren't in fact, dreaming.

Watching Jeremy disappear around the corner of the large brick building, Marion smiled and began her leisurely climb to the château, her new home. The air was filled with the fresh scents of spring and golden sunlight filtered through the branches of the trees, gently touching the wild flowers growing alongside the path. Occasionally the joyful sound of a bird song rang out from above.

Marion walked along, lighthearted and carefree, caught up in the beauty around her, marveling at all the sights and sounds. The orphanage and the different foster homes she had lived in had always been in the heart of the city. She had a special love for animals, and house plants flourished under her delicate care, but she had never had a chance to spend much time in the country. And from what she could see, she was going to love it. The leaves had so many different shapes, the velvety moss so many shades of green, a nearby stream murmured constantly in her ears. Life seemed filled with promise.

She reached a spot where several paths diverged. Jeremy had mentioned this spot, but she realized that because so much had been on her mind, she hadn't listened to him as carefully as she should have. Try as she might she couldn't recall which path she should take, so she took the one she thought would lead in the right direction. The path appeared to be a tunnel bathed in soft green light, but as she continued to walk it gradually became darker and darker. The forest became thicker, the trees seemed closer together and among the dark evergreens only rarely was there the splash of white of a birch tree. Rocks in strange formations looked like gnomes crouching in the shadows.

The path, which had been quite wide at its beginning, became narrow and the footing became slippery. More and more often, Marion found herself stumbling over a tree stump or root. The happiness she had felt earlier was dissipating quickly.

How long had she been walking? A glance at her watch told her that it had been an hour since she left Jeremy. By this time, she should have been close enough to the château at least to be able to see it. But there was no sign of any kind of clearing in the dense forest ahead. She soon realized that she had taken the wrong path, but she kept on walking, hoping that she soon would reach a clearing where she could get her bearings and perhaps see the château in the distance.

Now she was surrounded by trees growing so close together that their branches were intertwined. Now and then the shrill sound of a bird was heard, reminding Marion of fairy tales about birds that would lead you on and then disappear. *I might as well face it*, she thought. *I'm lost. This is ridiculous.*

She imagined what a good laugh they would all have about it when she finally did get back to the château. But first...she had to get back. Gathering up her courage, she kept going. "Every road leads somewhere," she kept telling herself. She spoke aloud, like a child afraid in the dark, feeling the beginning of terror. The sun was going down and it soon would be nightfall.

Quite suddenly the path she was following turned sharply downward and ended at what appeared at first

to be marshy terrain but was actually swampland
covered with various types of water plants through
which she could see the dark, murky water. Several
small streams fed into the pond and on the opposite side,
the main stream feeding it looked like an enormous
serpent. An ancient battered rowboat floated among the
bulrushes. There wasn't the slightest sound, not a squirrel, not a bird, only the whispering rustle of the wind
among the rushes. There was something distinctly sinister about the place. Marion turned and walked away
from it as quickly as she could.

The farther she walked, the more worried she became.
The path she was following now was uphill. Gradually it
widened until it finally opened onto a wild flower-
covered clearing where a large two-story house stood.
Attached to the house was a garage in which was parked
a powerful motorcycle. A dog was barking. Built of gray
stone, the house looked like a charming miniature of the
château, only less imposing and formal. A wisp of smoke
rising from one of several chimneys made Marion think
that someone must be home. *But who lives here*, Marion
wondered. It was the most beautiful house she had ever
seen and the way the last light illuminated its windows
cheered her.

For a brief moment she thought she caught a glimpse
of something red moving behind one of the windows on
the first floor. *Someone must be home*, she thought. The red
reminded her of something, someone she had seen only
recently. Was that the woman who was crying in Jeremy's office?

She crossed the clearing and knocked on the door of
the house. A man wearing a suede jacket and corduroy
trousers opened the door. Marion recognized him immediately as Leon Altamira, the manager Jeremy hated so
much.

At closer range Marion could see the haughty line of
the nose, the strong square jaw and piercing black eyes.
At first glance his hair seemed to be dark brown, but
actually, it was a deep shade of auburn. There was some-

thing wild about him...but something distinctly virile. Certainly he was attractive. He was keeping a firm hold on a dog with a shiny black coat and fierce eyes. The dog was barking furiously.

"Quiet, Satan!" he ordered.

The strong deep voice matched his physique very well. He looked at Marion and added, "Don't worry. Satan attacks only when I order him to do so."

He let go of the collar and the dog moved cautiously forward to sniff Marion. Apparently satisfied with the results of his investigation, he started to wag his tail.

Leon closed the door behind him, making Marion wonder if there was somebody inside. Could it really be Ida Somers? Marion remembered how upset the woman had been and what Jeremy had said earlier. Was Leon the man mysteriously referred to as involved in her "man problems"?

Marion didn't know what to say. She could see how a woman could be attracted and seduced by a man like Leon. He was so overpowering...and strong. As for Ida, she looked like the type of woman who ....

"Well?" Leon said curtly, shocking her out of her thoughts.

"I'm sorry to bother you...but, could you tell me how to get back to Grunberg?"

The man looked at her for a second, then threw back his head and started to laugh, revealing gleaming white teeth. "If I'm not mistaken, you're the famous Jeremy's fiancée."

Annoyed and slightly on the defensive, she replied, "That's right, I am Mr. Koster's fiancée."

"Why have you come to my house?" he asked, without taking his eyes off her.

Embarrassed, she explained that she had been taking the shortcut through the forest from the mill and had lost her way.

Again he laughed. "And I'm the one who's been chosen to help Mr. Koster's fiancée back onto the right road."

"It's not funny," said Marion indignantly.

She wondered why he was being so sarcastic and caustic. The man was upsetting her. With this kind of arrogance, she decided, he seemed better suited to heading a gang of thieves than holding the position of manager and gamekeeper. No wonder Jeremy couldn't stand him. His manners were abominable.

"No," he said. "That isn't the part that's funny. It's that you've come to *me* for help."

He was staring at her so boldly that Marion blushed.

"I couldn't see you very well yesterday," he continued. "I'll admit that Jeremy has made a good choice—I wouldn't have expected it of him. Are you wealthy, as well as everything else?"

Marion was shocked. First he had bluntly appraised her—and now he seemed to be suggesting that Jeremy wasn't marrying her for love, but for his own self-interest. Yet she was anything but rich. For what reason *but* love would Jeremy be marrying her?

"You're mistaken," she shot back coldly. "I haven't a cent to my name."

"Really?" He seemed baffled, as though her revelation had shattered all of his preconceived notions. He rubbed his chin and frowned in confusion. Then he made a vague gesture with one hand, as though waving away the issue for the moment in the knowledge that light would be shed on this mystery sooner or later.

Tears of anger came to Marion's eyes. She couldn't bear to listen to the implied contempt for Jeremy in everything this man said. She could well understand why Jeremy hated him. In only these few minutes she was reaching that point herself.

"I have to admit that you're something of a surprise," he said with a laugh. Once again he was wearing that exasperating smile. "And no doubt you're completely in awe of this 'perfect' gentleman." His laugh sounded more like a snort in its irony. "What a gullible little fool!" he muttered. "The human race definitely is not improving very much!"

Now his tone seemed to be a mixture of pity and

sarcasm. She looked at him with fury flashing in her eyes. This was a man who certainly knew how to infuriate people. Even Marion, who generally was very gentle, could feel every fiber of her being trembling in anger. She couldn't recall ever having felt this way before. She shouted with a passion even she was unaware she possessed. "You're...despicable! It's certainly easy to see why Jeremy hates you!"

Leon kept right on smiling, leaning nonchalantly in the doorway. "It just so happens that the feeling is mutual. I can't stand the sight of him, either. Two men who are as opposite as we are couldn't be anything else but enemies. Of course, I'm an absolute beast compared to the silver-tongued, well-mannered Jeremy."

Without attempting to answer she stood staring at him for a moment, finally having to lower her eyes before his piercing gaze. Exhausted by the walk and the fear of being lost in the forest, this very strange conversation was almost too much. She had just about reached the breaking point. Her heart was hammering in her chest and she felt her knees starting to give when a strong hand immediately grasped her arm.

"Please...don't pass out!" Leon said with a look of tender concern that took her by surprise. He was very strong, and held her up effortlessly.

"Let go of me," she protested, pulling her arm free. "I have to get back to the château."

"But you don't know how to get there."

"I'll find the way...somehow."

"It wouldn't be very nice of me to let you go wandering off on your own, now, would it?" In a much softer tone he added, "Please, don't be silly. Take hold of my arm and I'll go with you."

"I feel much better now, thank you."

Marion ignored his proferred arm and through sheer will forced herself to overcome her exhaustion. Walking with determination she followed Leon along a path in back of the house.

She was afraid he would start talking again and insult-

ing Jeremy, but he didn't. She was still shaking inwardly
with anger at his arrogance. He was a terrible man—
mean and rude. She could see that Jeremy was right
about him...and again she wondered about that woman
she had seen in Jeremy's office. She pitied her if she had
been hurt by this man.

Leon walked in silence followed closely by his dog. In
no time at all they arrived at the edge of the wood where
the château stood in all its splendor. Leon stopped. "You
shouldn't have any trouble from here," he said sarcastically. "I don't see any need to impose myself on you any
longer. Give my regards to Mrs. Koster...and do tell
Jeremy what good care I took of his fiancée. He's sure to
appreciate it."

Everything he said was touched with irony. Was he
always this way? With an effort Marion managed to
control herself and speak in a low voice.

"I believe I should be thanking you...."

"That isn't necessary. I wouldn't be the least bit
offended if you didn't. Good night. If you ever get lost
again, remember...I'm always at your service."

With an elaborate bow from the waist he wheeled
around and walked jauntily away, whistling, the dog
bounding after him. Marion felt troubled, as though this
man had cast a spell on her. Fighting a conflict of feelings
she had never experienced before she stood for a
moment and watched as the tall, handsome figure disappeared into the trees. Then she turned and started
toward the château.

Chapter 5

When Marion reached the château everything was quiet. She was glad; she didn't feel like talking to anyone. Going directly to her room, she dropped onto the love seat and in a few minutes was fast asleep.

It was dinnertime when she woke up. Hurriedly she washed, changed her clothes and brushed her hair before going downstairs to the dining room. Seated at the table in a high-backed chair, Isabel greeted her with a smile. Marion forced herself to return the smile and felt ashamed of herself for feeling so cold toward this woman who was her future husband's cousin. Before very long she would be her cousin too.

"Children," Mrs. Koster was saying, "we'd better start thinking about making arrangements to have the banns published. I know it's a nuisance, but it has to be done."

She paused and smiled before continuing.

"The road to happiness is never entirely smooth, you know. There are always a few troublesome details to make bumps and hollows."

"Fine, Martha," Jeremy agreed in a businesslike voice. "I thought we could go tomorrow."

Again Martha paused before turning to speak to Marion in a different tone.

"My dear child, I'm not planning to give a party to celebrate your wedding. I hope you won't mind a small group. My health isn't what it should be these days."

"Of course," Marion responded warmly. She glanced shyly toward Jeremy. "We want a small wedding anyway. We were hoping you wouldn't mind."

Martha reached across the table and took Marion's hand. "But I want it to be a wedding you will always treasure. I know the memory of that day will mean a great deal to you when you get to be my age."

There was such tender sadness in her voice that Marion found herself blinking back tears. The memory of her nightly dream came back to her. The guests were waiting in all their finery, their faces filled with expectation, only to become gradually more disappointed as the rumor spread that there would be no wedding.

Mrs. Koster took a jewel case from her pocket and handed it to Marion.

"This is your engagement present," she said. "I chose it for you from my own jewelry."

She opened the case and Marion was stunned to see an antique gold ring set with a large gleaming emerald surrounded by diamonds.

"This is really much too generous of you!" she murmured, shaking her head.

"Martha! You didn't tell me," Jeremy exclaimed, obviously taken aback by his stepmother's generosity.

"But Martha!" Isabel cried out, making a move that suggested that she wanted to grab the ring from Martha's hand.

"Can't I have my surprises, too?" Martha said playfully. "I think a lot of your future wife, Jeremy, and I want her to know it."

"Thank you," Marion whispered gently. "I don't know what to say."

"Don't say anything child...It's written in your beautiful eyes," Martha replied.

Not even in her wildest dreams had Marion ever imagined that she would own a piece of jewelry such a this. But then, she had never imagined that she would marry a man like Jeremy, either. "I couldn't possibly accept this," she said. "It's much too beautiful for me."

Mrs. Koster looked at the fine lines of the delicate face, the gray violet eyes, the generous contour of the young woman's lips.

"Unlike most young women of today, you're much too modest about yourself, Marion. You seem quite unaware that you are a very beautiful woman."

Marion sighed. "Not as beautiful as I'd like to be...for Jeremy." She stole a timid glance at her future husband. He looked displeased. Was he angry that she felt such things, and that she would say them to his stepmother?

Martha Koster burst out laughing. Marion was a little surprised to hear the crystal clear laughter; there was usually an aura of sadness around her.

"Yes," said the older woman, "Jeremy is handsome all right." She winked at her stepson. "But so was his father and I don't remember ever finding that to be any reason for me to have an inferiority complex! You must learn to be more sure of yourself...more aware of your own charm. In other words, don't be silly."

In a different tone, she continued.

"I'm delighted that you like this ring. It's a family heirloom. There's a history and a legend attached to it. The emerald came from India, where it was given to a Sayn prince by a fakir. It's supposed to bring happiness to the person who wears it without ever taking it off. I hope it works for you."

She smiled and gradually the skepticism left her face. In a quiet voice she murmured, "Of course, no one can vouch for the truth of such superstitions. So much of life remains a mystery to all of us. I scoffed at the power of that ring and have experienced much sorrow. Lucille refused to believe in it, too, and she died at twenty."

She stopped for a moment, appearing to be lost in her own memories. Then she shook her head as though to chase away the sad thoughts.

"Lucille?" Marion asked quietly.

"Lucille was my daughter. You remind me of her."
There was a moment's awkward silence, save for Isabel's
nervous handling of the silver and fine bone china.

"Put the ring on your middle finger, Marion. According to tradition, that's where it's supposed to be worn.
And you must never take it off. I want you to wear it in
the hope that it will prove to be a talisman of happiness
for you."

"You're very kind, Martha!" murmured Marion. "How
can I ever thank you?"

Mrs. Koster's voice was strangely rough as she replied. "Don't try to thank me. It's just possible that I'm
getting more pleasure from this ring simply by offering
it to you."

Marion suddenly realized that underneath that
appearance of always being slightly aloof, Mrs. Koster
was hiding extraordinary kindness and sensitivity.

"I have neither father nor mother. At least, I never
knew them...."

Despite the love she felt for Jeremy, Marion sometimes felt a great void in her heart, a kind of yearning for
something else. On an impulse that came from deep
within her, Marion got up from her chair and went to
Martha's side. Oblivious to Jeremy and Isabel, she gave
the older woman a warm hug and a kiss, wiping away the
tears that rolled down her cheeks.

"I'm so embarrassed," she said suddenly, straightening
up and returning to her chair, laughing at herself. She
glanced at Jeremy, who seemed strangely silent. Suddenly she was afraid that she might have acted out of
line. Mrs. Koster's warm eyes met hers.

"There's no reason to be embarrassed," she smiled,
seeming to understand Marion's sudden discomfort.

There was a moment's silence.

"Did you like our forest, my dear?" Martha Koster
asked, in an effort to put Marion at ease. "Did you have a
good walk?"

"It was marvelous at first." Marion sighed. "I loved the
trees, the fresh air, all the different smells, the birds
singing...and then I got lost."

"Lost?" Jeremy raised his eyebrows. "But I thought I described the route very carefully."

He seemed annoyed. Marion confessed that she had forgotten some of his instructions.

"At the crossroads known as Birds' Crossing, you were to take the path to the left. It leads directly to the château."

"I guess my sense of direction isn't very good. I took the path to the right," explained Marion, her tone apologetic. "But I did manage to get home okay anyway."

Marion paused. She didn't know if she should mention her meeting with Leon. If she did, she knew she would feel compelled to tell Jeremy everything Leon had said and she was afraid of upsetting him.

"You're not telling us the whole story," Isabel said suddenly with an accusing stare. "I saw you come back."

Marion looked across the table at Isabel, who was staring at her. Jeremy looked at Marion, a frown on his face.

"I have nothing to hide," Marion said as gracefully as she was able. "The path I finally took led me to Mr. Altamira's house. By the time I got there, I was completely exhausted. He showed me how to get home. As a matter of fact he walked along with me until I was out of the forest."

"I assume he invited you to come in so you could rest for a while?" asked Jeremy suspiciously.

Marion shook her head no. "Besides, I think there was someone there," she blurted out. "A woman—the one in your office."

Jeremy stared at Marion coldly, slowly digesting what she had just said. "That's interesting," he replied in a tone heavy with insinuation. He turned to his mother. "You see? I've been telling you all along that your manager is nothing but an uncivilized brute."

The hostility in his voice equaled the bitter sarcasm Marion remembered hearing in Leon's tone with every reference to Jeremy. She wondered what could have happened between the two men to bring about their hatred for each other. She looked at her fiancé and saw his elegant refinement, at the same time remembering the piercing eyes and wry smile so characteristic of Leon. Clearly, they were direct opposites. Could this explain their antagonism? Partly, perhaps.

"According to you, poor Leon will never be able to do anything right," said Mrs. Koster, her expression full of mischief. "He has a right to whatever guests he chooses. Besides, if he had invited Marion in, you wouldn't have liked that either. You're a bit sticky about everything being proper. You know it and I'm sure Leon knows it. Very likely, he was thinking precisely of that when he didn't invite Marion into his house."

"I don't believe for a minute that Altamira is concerned at all about such matters," said Jeremy. "It's far more likely that he just didn't want to show any kind of hospitality to my future bride."

Isabel, who had been sitting staring at Jeremy without saying a word, spoke up. "Altamira should have considered it an elementary duty to open his house and provide shelter to Marion. In view of his position, there would have been nothing improper about such a gesture."

Mrs. Koster looked at the old cousin and gently corrected her. "Leon is not a servant. Neither is he a slave. He's quite free to invite anyone he wishes into his house. Or, on the other hand, not invite anyone, if that is his wish. Marion tells us that he walked with her until she was out of the forest. He didn't have to do that. It was an act of courtesy, and we should be grateful to him."

Aware that she had made a blunder, Isabel lowered her face to look down at the table in front of her. Jeremy put down the glass he had been holding in his hand, not daring to interfere. After an awkward moment of silence he looked at his stepmother and smiled.

"Well, I can see that I'm never going to get anywhere criticizing Altamira. I might as well get used to the idea." In the same pleasant smiling tone, he added, "Anyway, Marion got home safely and Altamira was correct with her. That's the main thing."

"He couldn't have been more proper," said Marion

emphatically. She said nothing about Leon's incredible sarcasm or his obvious dislike for Jeremy. To change the direction of the conversation she turned to something else.

"In spite of it all I did get to see the forest. The trees are magnificent and there are so many other interesting things. Those rocks, for instance, which seem to have human forms. I also happened upon a pond that seemed somewhat sinister."

She stopped talking at seeing the reaction to her words. Mrs. Koster's smile suddenly fell from her face. Isabel opened her mouth but made no sound. The maid who was taking away the dishes froze in her tracks. After a moment Jeremy began to speak very quietly.

"It's called the Green Pond," he explained, "and is connected to an underground river. The terrain all around is very marshy, of course, so it isn't very safe to get too close to it. You're quite right in saying it's a sinister place."

The matter-of-fact tone of his voice dispelled the sudden gloom. The maid resumed her duties, Isabel sighed and took a tablet to aid her digestion. Only Mrs. Koster remained pale and tense. Jeremy went on, still smiling.

"Next time you want to take a walk in the woods, I'll offer you a sack of white pebbles as well as a detailed map of the area, showing all the paths."

Marion returned his smile. "Thank you," she said simply.

She realized that in speaking about the pond, she had brought up a subject that would better have been left unmentioned. Had something happened there? And why was Mrs. Koster so upset by it?

The remainder of the evening passed without incident. Isabel was doing her utmost to please in order to be forgiven for having blundered. And while managing to appear involved in the somewhat shallow conversation Mrs. Koster seemed to be forcing, Marion was thinking about the events of the day.

She thought about the Green Pond. She recalled the

desperation on the face of the woman in the red dress
and thought of Jeremy's explanation of it...and then
the strange telephone call. She recalled the mocking
expression on Leon's face. His sarcastic comments continued to ring in her ears.

She couldn't explain why, but for some reason she was
quite convinced that the "someone" in Leon's cottage
had been Ida, the girl who had been crying in Jeremy's
office. But what was she doing there? What was the link
between her and Leon? Was there any connection
between the girl's tears and the hatred between Jeremy
and Leon?

The whole situation was very intriguing. Marion
found herself filled with questions...and a growing
determination to find the answers.

Chapter 6

At some point during the night Marion was awakened by the touch of something warm and silky against her arm. When she opened her eyes, two phosphorescent orbs were staring at her, inches from her face. Of course it was Tiger. For the time being, at least, he had chosen Marion's bed as the one place he wanted to sleep. Charmed by the cat's display of affection, she cuddled him in her arms and went back to sleep. In the morning he had his share of breakfast milk and went on his way.

When Marion went downstairs a little later, the first person she saw was Isabel.

"Martha isn't feeling very well this morning. She'll be staying in bed until noon, when she expects to go into town with you and Jeremy to publish the banns. I'm just taking her a cup of tea and the newspapers now. She doesn't want to be disturbed."

After a pause she added, "Jeremy is at the factory. He said to tell you that he'll see you at noon. Until then you can go out for a walk, or read, if you like. On the same floor as your room there's a library. I think you'll find it very well stocked. A new book is added every week."

Feeling a little helpless in this enormous house where she felt like a stranger when Jeremy wasn't with her,

Marion returned to her room and stood looking out the window. The beautiful weather of the previous day had been replaced by a thick mist that obliterated the scenery. It was definitely not the kind of day to go out for a walk. Marion decided to have a look at the library. As she was leaving the room, Tiger appeared and started rubbing against her legs. Then he started to walk away, but stopped to look back as if inviting her to follow him.

Marion decided to see where he would lead. She followed him along the hall and around a corner into another hallway, then down a steep flight of stairs. At the bottom of the steps, the cat stood on his hind legs and pushed on a door with his front paws. It was obvious that he wanted her to open it for him.

A little hesitantly Marion knocked. She heard a faint, "come in" from within. She turned the handle and the door opened onto a bright room. French doors looked out on a small courtyard where several pigeons were feeding on the ground. Through the window could be seen a small garden and in the distance, through the mist, the edge of the forest. Marion realized that she was on the other side of the château. There were two old women in the room. One was knitting, the other pouring coffee. From the doorway Marion recognized Marguerite, the old servant.

"Excuse me," Marion said. "Tiger led me here and let me know that he wanted me to open your door for him."

"He's clever, that one!" she said. "He knows exactly how to get what he wants. Come in, come in."

The room was filled with the fragrant aromas of coffee, herb sachets and plants. It was plainly furnished with the exception of one chair covered in bright blue velvet, which Marguerite indicated to Marion.

There was no embarrassment in her greeting, nor in the way she introduced the other woman.

This is my friend Beth," she said simply. "We practically grew up together."

Beth, as plump as Marguerite was skinny, smiled. "Yes. We've been arguing with each other for years over just about everything...even our boyfriends."

"It's true!" agreed Marguerite. "But we've always been the best of friends, just the same. We both came to work at Grunberg at the same time...a very long time ago. To show her gratitude to us for having served her for so long, the mistress gave us each an apartment of our own on the ground floor of the château. She allowed us to bring in our own furniture and we can do our own cooking. This is my apartment and Beth's is next door. We're the only two in the whole château with this kind of arrangement."

Marion could see very clearly that they were thankful to Mrs. Koster as well as proud of being especially privileged, which set them apart from the other servants.

"How long have you been here then?" Marion asked, charmed by these two old friends.

"Oh, we were already at Grunberg when the mistress married her first husband, Mr. de Steyer," Marguerite answered eagerly. "That was more than forty years ago."

She stopped to give Marion a cup of coffee, also pouring some for Beth and herself. Then she continued. "Poor Mr. de Steyer died very soon after they were married—it was only after one year I believe—leaving the mistress a young widow with an infant called Lucille to take care of."

Beth interrupted with a question. "That was the year Sebastian Viry was courting both of us, remember?"

"Yes," said Marguerite. "And he wound up marrying a girl from the village."

"And there was José Henequin, with the curly hair."

"Yes!"

"And we both stayed single," concluded Beth, a little wistfully.

It was amusing for Marion to listen to the two reminiscing about their past, their long lost loves. At first, she thought she might get Marguerite to tell her some of the legends of the region, but now she preferred just to let both of them ramble on about whatever they wanted to tell her.

"To get back to the mistress," Marguerite was saying,

"she was so young and so beautiful, many men fell in love with her. But she had her daughter, whom she was devoted to, and none of the men interested her—she would have nothing to do with any of them. Until Emile Koster, that is. And then the sparks did fly! She married him very shortly after she met him. He had just become the owner of the knitting mill. He was very handsome. Well, I don't have to describe him to you. Jeremy is the spitting image of his father. It might have been said that as a husband, he wasn't the best choice the mistress could have made. . .a man with no fortune, no name, but she didn't care."

The old woman seemed to drift off into her own thoughts for a moment. Then she continued.

"You see, the mistress married Mr. de Steyer just to please her family. He wasn't wealthy, but he was from a noble family. Such arrangements were often made among the rich and titled people then. And he was a good man. But it was definitely for love that she married her second husband, Emile Koster. You should have seen the expression in her eyes when they were together."

Marion nodded. She had gathered from the way Martha had talked about Emile that their love had been very strong. She loved his memory still, judging from the way her eyes lighted up whenever she mentioned him.

"Oh, yes, there wasn't any doubt that she loved him," Beth agreed. "Mind you, there was one person who was quite shocked when Emile married the mistress—Isabel."

From the way she spoke and from the change of expression on Marguerite's face, it was quite clear that Isabel had never succeeded in gaining the affection of these two old servants.

Marguerite was nodding her head in agreement.

"Yes, she had always been in love with her cousin. But he never gave her a second look! After his first wife died, Isabel thought she was going to to have him all to herself. She moved in with him on the pretext that he needed someone to look after his house and Jeremy, who was a boy at that time. I suppose she was hoping that Emile would eventually marry her."

Marion started. She wondered if that was why Isabel seemed so unhappy. And was she jealous of her own happiness, marrying Jeremy? She longed to ask these two women all they knew about her future family since Jeremy was strangely reluctant to give her any details.

"That's why Isabel had to go to the hospital after Martha and Emile married," Marguerite went on. "They said it was illness, but a nurse at the hospital was a friend of ours and she told us what it really was. Don't tell anyone, but Isabel was said to be what they called...what was it, Beth?"

"Psychotic...that was it."

"We never could figure out what that means, but she would act very strange and even violent every now and then and have to go to the hospital. Lots of times they had her on heavy drugs, remember, Beth?"

"Oh, all those pills! It wasn't easy keeping them all straight."

"Anyway, I think the mistress thought it was her fault that Isabel had to go to the hospital. That her marrying Emile caused it all. We think that's why she keeps her here still, even if she is so peculiar."

The keen-eyed servants hadn't missed a thing. Both of these women seemed very aware of something even Mrs. Koster chose to ignore. What she had just heard confirmed Marion's first impression of Isabel.

Marguerite continued to relate her memories. "Then, quite suddenly, Mr. Koster died. Poor Mrs. Koster was left again, this time with her husband's son, Jeremy, as well as her own daughter, Lucille. Jeremy was only two or three years younger than Lucille as I recall."

There was no outside noise coming into the room. The normal activities of daily living seemed separate from the apartment, so filled was it with memories of the past.

"Lucille grew up to be a beautiful young woman. She was a brunette, tall and slender like the pictures of models you see in magazines. And she had a voice like

music! She married the man she loved, Maurice Reinfeld, and they had a daughter, whom they called Josina.
The christening was the last party ever held at the
château. So terrible. . . . The young couple was killed in a
car accident."

"I know . . . Jeremy told me," murmured Marion. The
evening before, she had been quite upset not to have
known that Martha had had a daughter. Her ignorance
had caused her to ask, innocently enough, a question
that had pained Mrs. Koster. She didn't want that to
happen again. After dinner when she and Jeremy were
sitting alone in front of the fireplace in the living room,
she had demanded more information from him. And she
had gotten a bit, but from what she was hearing today,
she knew he hadn't revealed all. Why hadn't Jeremy told
her about Josina, the granddaughter? "What happened
to their little girl?"

Marguerite's voice was somber now and she heaved a
great sigh before answering.

"Another tragedy."

Aware that Marion was completely caught up in the
story, she paused, being a true storyteller who knows
how to create maximum effect.

"The baby was just learning to how to walk. Felicia, a
young governess, had taken her for a ride in the push-
cart through the forest. Well, like most young girls,
Felicia had a lover. She would often meet him near the
Green Pond. One day she took Josina there . . . and that's
when it happened—although nobody knows exactly
what *did* happen. The governess said that the baby was
sleeping and she went for a walk with her boyfriend. She
claimed that they hadn't gone far from the pond, but it
must have been far enough for the baby to be out of her
sight. When she came back a little later the cart was
overturned and . . . empty. At first she thought the little
girl had managed to get out of the cart, but they couldn't
find her anywhere. Crying and hysterical, the governess
ran back to the château to get help. A search was organ-
ized, but the baby was never found. Finally the authori-

ties said that the baby must have drowned in the pond."

Marion pressed her hand to her mouth, her eyes filled with horror and pity. Now she understood why what she had said about the Green Pond had upset Mrs. Koster.

Her voice a monotone by this time, Marguerite continued.

"They dragged the pond for days, but the body was never found. It was decided that it must have been carried away by the underground river and probably never would be found."

"It must have been...horrible...for Mrs. Koster," murmured Marion.

"Yes," replied Marguerite. "It was a catastrophe."

"*Madam* has never been the same," murmured Beth. "Everything happened so quickly. First her husband died, then her daughter and granddaughter...." Beth's voice revealed an intense sorrow that showed how much she cared for Mrs. Koster.

Marion could picture in her mind the kind of life the mistress of Grunberg must have led. She had learned more from these two old servants than she would ever have dared to ask anyone else. "Now she has only Jeremy."

Marguerite nodded her head.

"Yes. She cares for him, there's no doubt about that...but her blood doesn't run in his veins."

Turning her wrinkled face with its bright, piercing eyes to Marion she went on to explain that she meant.

"*Madam* comes from a very aristocratic family. The Sayn princes ruled these parts for centuries and they made sure that it would stay that way. Shortly after Josina died Mrs. Koster made plans to leave her fortune to Jeremy. He was, after all, the only family she had left. But her lawyers discovered something in the ancient deeds that made that impossible. The Sayn princes had ruled that if no blood relative could be found, the property was to go to the state to be turned into a park."

Marion was shocked. Why hadn't Jeremy told her this? He had implied that they would always live at the

château. She couldn't believe that he wouldn't have
mentioned these facts to her. "But you must be mistaken!" she cried bewilderment in her voice. "Jeremy
would have said something to me."

"Oh, dear, I know I shouldn't have started talking,"
Marguerite exclaimed. "I do get carried away, I'm afraid.
And now we'll get in trouble."

Beth leaned over to Marion to explain. "You see, no one
knows we know all this. They forget about us sometimes
and we'll hear things when we bring in tea, or—" Beth
paused, an embarrassed twinkle in her eye. "Or they'll
leave open letters around."

"Beth! You shouldn't tell. . . ."

But Marion only laughed, putting the old friends at
ease again. "Don't worry. I'll keep your secret. I won't
tell." She resolved to ask Jeremy to tell her the details. He
would tell her all, of that she was sure.

"Well, in any case, Mrs. Koster is sure that there must
be some blood relatives, somewhere, and that when she
dies, they'll eventually be found. She'll leave something
to Jeremy, of course, but the major part of the estate, the
land and the châteaus in Belgium and Germany will have
to go to Sayn blood relatives."

"But let's not talk of such troublesome things. When is
the wedding?"

"Saturday after next."

"So soon! Oh Marguerite, won't it be beautiful!"

"Oh, yes. Do you have your dress ready?" Marguerite
asked.

"The day after tomorrow I have to go back to Paris to
pick it up. My wedding dress and trousseau are being
made there. I designed the dress myself—I hope it will
turn out."

"How exciting. Beth and I are quite good with a needle,
so if you need any alterations made just let us know."

"Did you do the embroidery and needlepoint?" Marion
had been noticing the numerous examples of fine nee-
dlework displayed on pillows, furniture and framed on
the walls.

"Oh, yes. Of course, over the years, it does mount up."

"But they are so beautiful, the most beautiful work I have ever seen. I wonder, would you be interested in embroidering my wedding dress? I know that there won't be much time, but...."

"Of course, we'd love to," they nodded and murmured in unison, their faces beaming with the compliment and the excitement of the project.

"There has been a good deal of sadness at Grunberg," Marguerite added slowly. "It's about time there was a little joy around here!"

"It certainly is about time," sighed Beth.

The two old women looked at each other. In the hazy morning light Tiger was perched on a chair, his paws curled beneath him, as motionless as a sphinx, appearing to be deep in thought.

Marion had begun by expecting to hear legends and ended up listening to facts...facts far more interesting to her than fiction.

Chapter 7

It was almost noon when Marion left her new friends Marguerite and Beth, after several cups of coffee and more information than she really, deep in her heart, wanted to hear. Yet she was glad. Except for her friendship with Martha, which she treasured more and more, she felt a stranger in this family and this house. Now some of the mystery was gone, and she knew that she would be better able to understand those around her—especially Isabel, who had puzzled her. Perhaps now, she could respond to her with more understanding and sympathy.

Approaching the dining room, where she expected to find Martha and Isabel eating their lunch, she heard Jeremy's deep and commanding voice.

"I'm afraid that I can't take too much time off today. We're having some problems with the union and I have to get back as soon as I can. Why don't we skip lunch and get on with it."

Marion's heart stopped. She was glad to hear his voice. Since they had arrived from Paris they had hardly seen each other. It was such a contrast to the constant attention Jeremy had showered on her before they had become engaged. Yet she was nervous, too. She had learned some very strange bits of information from Marguerite and Beth, and although she hoped that they were mistaken, she knew they were honest.

"Hello," Marion said warmly as she came into the room. She gave Jeremy a welcoming kiss on the cheek. Martha was there and so was Isabel.

"Well, I guess we have to get on with it," Martha said with a smile of resignation. "I wasn't feeling so well this morning. I was thinking about staying home and letting the two of you go on without me, but I think I'll pull myself together and tag along. It might be more awkward for you if I didn't, I'm afraid. Jeremy, you don't know the reverend, do you?"

"The Reverend Mr. Lenotre?" His stepmother nodded. "No."

"Well, then. I'd better at least introduce you."

After a short spell of organizing the chauffeur and finding their coats and wraps, they were all ready to go. Much to Marion's dismay Isabel also climbed into the car and sat in the front seat next to the chauffeur. For some reason she had been determined to come along and Mrs. Koster had finally relented.

Going down the hill, Marion squeezed Jeremy's hand. She, Jeremy, Martha and the cook, who had to go into town for some food, had all been squeezed into the back seat of the elegant Mercedes. Somehow it wasn't the quiet and romantic outing that Marion had hoped for, but at least it was a step toward their getting married.

It was a beautiful sunny day. A soft wind blew gently, barely causing the tops of the evergreens to sway.

Jeremy glanced at Marion and smiled. She looked so fragile beside him, so delicate. Her fine curls made a dark, glowing halo around her perfectly shaped ivory face. She held her head proudly; although her bearing was kind and thoughtful, an inner strength and sensitivity showed in her fine bones and clear gray eyes. She wasn't a dramatic woman, but, on close examination, she would undoubtedly be one of the most beautiful in any gathering.

After dropping the cook off in the market place they went on to the church where they were going to be married. There weren't many to choose from in the small town. Jeremy had never attended any church so they had decided to be married in the church Mrs. Koster was an active member of. At the front door they were met by a young curate with deep blue eyes and a serene expression.

Martha Koster shook his hand. "My dear Reverend Lenotre, I'd like to introduce you to my son Jeremy, and my future daughter-in-law Marion Charles. You know Isabel, of course."

The curate nodded and shook hands with everyone, then showed them into a room that was furnished in simple rustic furniture.

As soon as they were all seated Mrs. Koster explained the reason for their visit.

"Well, as you've no doubt gathered by now, I am most delighted to say that we've come to make the necessary arrangements for this young couple to be married. I'm sure you're already aware that there is to be a wedding."

The priest smiled. "Rumor—in this case, by way of my maid Anne—has indeed advised me. Anne seems to know absolutely everything that goes on in these parts and considers it her duty to keep me informed."

His smile disappeared suddenly, to be replaced by a serious expression. Joining his hands together, he spoke slowly. "Marriage always has been meant to be a very serious thing, but I'm afraid it doesn't mean very much to some people. Nowadays there are many who don't take it seriously at all—any more than they respect the dogmas of the church, or even the ten commandments."

His eyes moved back and forth from Marion to Jeremy, finally coming to rest on Jeremy. Conscious of his duties as a priest, he made much the same speech to all couples who came to talk to him about their wish to be married and ask for his blessing of the union.

"My role as a priest is to remind people of these things."

"You may rest assured, reverend," said Jeremy, "that both my fiancée and I understand very well that marriage is a serious business."

"You have definitely decided and are quite sure of your feelings?"

"Very definitely," said Jeremy.

There was some discussion about the date and the ceremony, which Marion and Jeremy wanted to keep as simple as possible, then they thanked the reverend, promising to contact him soon about further arrangements. The group then headed for the city hall, which was only a short distance away from the church.

The coming marriage between Marion and Jeremy must have been causing a stir among the townspeople. All along the way, curtains on front windows of the houses could be seen to move ever so slightly and one could feel that eyes were peering from behind the curtains as people tried to get a look at the future bride.

Without warning, Ida, the young girl from the factory, came out of a side street and headed straight toward the group. Suddenly, she stopped and stared intently at Jeremy with wild desperation in her blue eyes. Marion glanced at Jeremy and saw his frown. In the next instant his face took on an impersonal mask, cold and distant.

But if it had been her intention to speak to Jeremy about something, Ida must have changed her mind. In a moment she had disappeared around the corner.

Marion's eyes followed her until she was out of sight. Had the young woman appeared just to make her presence felt?

When they reached the city hall, they found the mayor waiting for them. He got up from his desk and pompously greeted them. When everyone was seated to his satisfaction, he went back to his desk and sat down beneath the bust of the statue representing the Republic.

After his secretary had finished taking down all the necessary information, he put his elbows on the desk and leaned forward, smiling. "So, Jeremy, you've finally decided to settle down. We were beginning to think you were never going to get married. Of course, a lot of people will be surprised to learn that you had to go all the way to Paris to find a wife."

There seemed to be an unplesant meaning underlying his words and it occurred to Marion that he was probably echoing the feelings of many of the people behind those curtains.

"I chose the woman I wanted to share my life with to be my wife," replied Jeremy. "And you can tell anyone who may be surprised that I really don't much care what they think."

"Why, of course," the mayor said in a tone that clearly meant just the opposite.

Jeremy fixed the mayor with a steady gaze until the man lowered his eyes. Then he spoke, his voice cold. "I must say you have a somewhat odd way of offering your congratulations."

"Why, Jeremy, of course I congratulate you."

With a brief nod in Marion's direction, he added, "In less than two weeks, Miss Charles, you and your fiancé will be man and wife. . . that is, assuming there will be no objections or opposition to the marriage."

Marion looked at the mayor with fear in her eyes. Why was he talking like this? The mayor's words seemed filled with a kind of evil foreboding and the young woman was confused. Then Isabel, who hadn't been saying a word, suddenly got to her feet and spoke with ill-concealed hostility.

"Just what's that supposed to mean, Robert? You've always been an old fool. What possible opposition could there be to this marriage?"

Her normally lifeless eyes were burning with fury. "And I'd like to see anyone try to stop it!"

Completely baffled, Marion sat staring at the old woman. This marriage seemed to mean a lot to Isabel. Yet she never seemed warm at all toward Marion. Indeed, Marion observed, she was often cold and hostile.

Marion thought about her conversation earlier that

morning with Marguerite and Beth. Was Isabel still an "unbalanced" woman? Did she still have problems? Perhaps there was no explanation for her odd behavior, being violently in favor of the marriage one minute and cool and even hostile toward Marion the rest of the time. Marion was beginning to see that Isabel was someone she would have to endure and put up with, just as Martha apparently did.

In a calm soothing voice, Jeremy spoke to get things back into their proper perspective. "Come, come, Isabel, don't get so excited. I'm sure Robert didn't have anything in the back of his mind when he mentioned the possibility of opposition. It's merely a question of legal procedure."

The sunlight coming through the window highlighted his hair and lent extraordinary definition to his profile. No one could remain insensitive to Jeremy's incredible good looks. Isabel looked at him with admiration in her eyes and once again, Marion felt very fortunate that he had chosen her.

"Of course," the mayor agreed. "It's something we always say." In an effort to appear a little more amiable he added, "It should be quite a celebration at Grunberg...such a long time it's been since there was one! The last time was in honor of little Josina's baptism, wasn't it, Martha?"

Mrs. Koster turned pale and didn't answer.

As they filed out of the city hall, Marion felt relieved and took Jeremy's arm. The visit to the priest and the mayor left her with uneasy feelings. She was beginning to see that her marriage to Jeremy didn't seem to inspire a great deal of enthusiasm. Undoubtedly, both the priest and the mayor would have preferred that he marry a local woman. Some wealthy heiress, perhaps, rather than a simple working girl from Paris, a girl who had been raised in an orphanage. It was entirely possible that they saw her as a conniving fortune hunter. In her innocence Marion had always imagined country people to be simple and openhearted. She was quickly discovering that this just wasn't so. Here, just like everywhere else, there were mysteries.

Suddenly her thoughts turned to Ida. The young girl's face haunted her as though it were the face of a blond ghost dressed in red. She knew very well that she was being foolish, paying so much attention to a stranger, but she couldn't help herself. Why did she find every encounter with Ida so troublesome? She couldn't explain it, but it seemed to Marion that the young woman was quite desperate about something... and was asking for help. Marion would have welcomed the opportunity to speak to her, console her. And she would like to know if she had indeed been in Leon's house that day she had been lost in the forest.

One thing led to another, and she began to think about the manager, Altamira. She could still see that volatile face, the deep eyes and savage smile. And she could hear his sarcastic remarks.

She had become so obsessed by her thoughts of these two people that she had forgotten that she was soon to become Jeremy's wife. Nothing else should have mattered, of course... and yet, she was not feeling as happy as she should. Without understanding at all why, her heart was heavy with uneasy feelings. For some reason the whole procedure had become rather unpleasant and there was an air of mystery surrounding everything. Was she being overly suspicious and nervous? She thought of the vivid and troubling nightmare that had been jolting her from a sound sleep every night. Try as she might she had been unable to shake off her feeling of unease. Perhaps it was her nerves, the new surroundings, the excitement of getting married and all the new friends and family that were making her so touchy. *It's probably only natural, after all*, she reminded herself.

She felt Jeremy's arm tense and he seemed to jump almost imperceptibly. Marion looked up, having been absentmindedly staring at the sidewalk as they waited for their chauffeur to drive up.

On the far side of the square, sitting on a park bench,

she saw the vivid profile of Ida in her loose red dress. Suddenly something made Marion start. Ida was sitting peacefully, her hands folded primly in her lap.

"Is Ida pregnant, Jeremy?" Marion whispered. Martha and Isabel were sitting on a sidewalk bench not far from them.

"So I gather," Jeremy answered curtly.

Ida turned toward them, waved and smiled, and walked off.

What was that all about, Marion wondered. It seemed that the more answers she found, the more questions there were.

"You can see why I have little respect for Leon Altamira, Marion," Jeremy added in an icy voice.

"You mean he...?"

"I don't want to talk about it."

Marion fell silent, somewhat ashamed for having wanted to know about something that was really none of her business, and yet also a bit angry for having been cut off so abruptly by Jeremy. Once again she thought about all the things she had learned about Jeremy's family—things that he should have told her. When was she going to have a chance to ask him about the inheritance? Was it always going to be this way?

She was determined not to allow her questions go unanswered if not unheard.

"Why do you suppose the mayor made such a point of mentioning possible opposition?" she asked as they all climbed back into the car. Perhaps his words would have had much less impact had they not reminded her of her dream and the dreaded fear she seem unable to shake.

"No particular reason," Jeremy reassured her. "Just a legal technicality, as I said before." He paused to look at her. "But you seem to be inordinately bothered by it."

"It does bother me," she murmured.

"Well, you mustn't let it. There's no reason to be bothered."

"That man never had a penny to his name," Isabel snorted, her tone contemptuous. "And even then he was always creating some kind of embarrassment! Now that he's the mayor, he thinks he's so superior. The only thing to do is ignore him, no matter what he says."

With a quick glance at Isabel, Mrs. Koster spoke up. "I can't imagine what could have come over you to say what you said. You must try to restrain yourself."

Isabel simply smiled.

Jeremy grasped his fiancée's hand a little more firmly. "Why don't we just forget the whole thing? There isn't anything in the world that could prevent us from being happy. Right, darling?"

Jeremy was leaning toward her, his lips curved in the familiar expression of tenderness, but somehow as she looked into his eyes, Marion could feel the love in her heart become a little less secure.

Chapter 8

They dropped Jeremy off at the factory and headed back to the château. As Mrs. Koster got out of the car she said, "I know it's still quite early, but I think I'll go and lie down for a while. Making these arrangements has worn me out. Do you mind, Marion? Can you find something to do to pass the time until Jeremy gets home?"

Marion hesitated. She didn't feel like shutting herself in her room and she was definitely not interested in staying downstairs with Isabel.

"Maybe I'll take a walk in the forest," she murmured. She was feeling a little depressed—maybe a walk would make her feel better.

"Good idea," approved Mrs. Koster as they walked through the carved oak front doors. "But this time, don't get lost," she admonished affectionately.

"I'll follow the map Jeremy made for me."

"Well, don't wander off too far," cautioned the older woman, putting her arm around Marion's shoulders. "If you're not used to the country it's easy to lose direction, and it gets dark very quickly in the woods."

"Don't worry, I won't," Marion added, holding up her right hand with the emerald ring on it. "I'm protected now."

Mrs. Koster shook her head, an expression of tenderness lighting her face. "Yes...you *are* a dear," she whispered to herself. "Well," she continued, her voice louder, "if you change your mind, you might like to take a look at the rennovations in the west wing. It's time to start thinking about how you will want it decorated. They'll be ready to begin the finishing touches soon."

"Oh, Jeremy is looking after that. I think he has hired someone in Paris to design it." Deep down she had wondered whether Jeremy trusted her to pick out tasteful designs. He was very particular about certain things. Marion knew he would insist on the best, but still, she would have preferred to have had something to say about it. Besides, she was eager to see how it was coming along. After all, it would be her home in less than two weeks. But Jeremy was firm—he would tell her nothing.

"Jeremy wants to show it to me himself," she explained. "He insists on surprising me."

"Well, I'm not about to interfere with *that*," Martha laughed, opening the door to her private suite on the ground floor. "Have a pleasant afternoon, dear one. I'll look forward to hearing about your adventures this evening."

MARION CLIMBED THE STAIRS and got out the map Jeremy had made for her. She had no wish to go back to the eerie Green Pond. After carefully scrutinizing the map, she decided to take one of the paths that would keep her close to the château. From Jeremy's sketch, she saw that there was a brook meandering to the south and what seemed to be a small bridge and a teahouse close by. The path leading to it looked easy to follow; there were no forks, or too many bends to disturb her sense of direction. Just in case however, she decided to give Marguerite a note for Jeremy telling him where she was going and promising that she would be back before dusk.

The air was warm and pleasant along the shadowy path of the forest. From time to time Marion could hear small animals moving in the underbrush, or squirrels leaping from branch to branch overhead.

The day was bright and the air had a cool edge when she started out. As the day wore on and the sun climbed higher, however, Marion began to feel too warm. She had no difficulty following the path—it was well worn and easy to see. She was delighted after a time first to hear and then to see the clear, lively stream she had been looking for.

She stooped to feel the water. It was cool, but she was hot, and she yearned to splash in the stream, to feel the water running over her feet. She found a large, sun-warmed boulder to sit on, rounded smooth by the water. She slipped off her overblouse, shoes and stockings and stepped into the stream.

The shock of the mountain water took her breath away, raising goose bumps on her exposed shoulders and arms. She was wearing an inexpensive cotton dress, something she had bought in Paris before she had met Jeremy, yet it was one of her favorites. In the woods, at least, she could wear what she wanted and do as she pleased.

Soon she was used to the cold water and she kicked her feet delightedly over the pink-and-brown pebbles. The path followed the course of the stream, and she decided to continue on her way following its meandering route. She could come back for her clothes later.

Feeling more relaxed, she walked and splashed, jumping at times from rock to rock. All of a sudden she heard the snap of dried twigs. She looked up to see the tall figure of Leon Altamira standing on the path, staring at her. His dog was at his side, tensed to attack on command.

They looked at each other for a moment in silence. Inexplicably, Marion felt frightened. How long had he been watching her? She waited for him to speak, to say something, but he only stood there, watching her with a curious expression. Embarrassed and not knowing what to do, Marion climbed out of the stream and onto the path. She longed to go back for her clothes.

"H-hi..." Marion stammered, pushing fine wisps of curls out of her eyes. "I...I...." She stopped, not knowing what to say.

"I hope I didn't frighten you," Leon said, his deep black eyes taking her in.

Marion simply shrugged. "Not at all."

He threw back his head and laughed, showing his beautiful teeth. "You're not telling the truth. You look like a lamb that has just walked into the wolf's den."

Noticing her embarrassment, Leon continued in a more careful tone. "I'm sorry. I believe I didn't show myself to be as polite as I might have the first time we met and I want you to know that I regret it. Good manners are very important...especially in the company of a beautiful woman."

His tone became slightly less formal as he added, "To tell you the truth, my hostility had nothing to do with you personally."

"But it was directed at Jeremy's fiancée, wasn't it?"

"Precisely. I see that you did understand. Allow me to congratulate you on your clairvoyance."

He was so unpredictable. He certainly had the ability to upset her. Her initial reaction was to turn back, but after hesitating for a moment she decided to keep on walking. In no time at all the manager was at her side.

"You understood what it was all about, all right. But, after all, it really isn't your fault that I dislike Jeremy so much."

This conversation was making no sense at all. She should have brought it to a halt then and there and turned around to go back to the château without any explanation. However she didn't. Instead she asked a question, her voice trembling slightly.

"What is this thing between you and Jeremy? Why do you hate each other so much?"

He did not answer directly, and when he did he spoke in a vague tone. "It's a hatred that appears to be mutual, isn't it?"

"Yes," she agreed. "But what brought it about? Did Jeremy do something wrong? Did he cause you some kind of a problem?"

No sooner had she spoken than she realized that she

had inadvertently assumed that her fiancé was responsible for the feud. In an effort to correct this impression she added, "It can't be all that serious, surely."

He looked at her in silence for a moment before replying in a very calm voice. "My reasons, believe me, are perfectly valid. But I prefer to keep them to myself."

She realized that she wasn't going to find out anything more about it and sighed in frustration. A few moments went by. The dog was walking at his master's feet, his ears were up, very alert, listening for any unusual sounds. After an awkward pause Leon spoke again. "May I ask a question, now? Of course, you don't have to answer if you'd rather not. As the future wife of Jeremy Koster, are you happy?"

"Of course," she replied.

He persisted. *"Really* happy?"

She stopped on the path and looked at him defiantly. This man seemed able to bring out an aggressiveness in her that seemed totally alien to her nature.

"Yes, I'm really happy. Jeremy loves me and I love him. Nothing makes a woman happier than being able to love and at the same time to know that she is loved in return. Perhaps you don't know what it means to really love someone."

"I might have known at one time," he said bitterly. "But I prefer to forget about it. My expectations, perhaps, are a little too naive. I am a simple man at heart, you see."

With a strange look on his face he added, "But, life is never simple. Sometimes it can be incredibly complicated...and I'm always surprised at the ease with which young women seem to fall in love."

Marion's face flushed with anger. Leon seemed to be insinuating that she had fallen in love too quickly...that she had fallen for Jeremy, a rich and handsome man, like a silly schoolgirl. She found it totally unacceptable that Leon seemed to feel free to speak to her in such a way. She loved Jeremy. True, there were vast differences in their backgrounds, and Jeremy was not a man who found it easy to talk about his problems. But when they were married this would change. He would become much more outgoing, much better able to share his feelings with her, and their love for each other would continue to grow for the rest of their lives.

Marion looked at Leon, her eyes dark with anger. She wanted to tell him, explain to him, convince him of what she really felt for Jeremy.

"Leon—" she began.

"As heir to Mrs. Koster's fortune," he interrupted curtly, changing the subject altogether, "which, it would seem, is considerable, your fiancé will be a very wealthy man one day."

Not fully understanding the reason behind such a remark, Marion protested. "Jeremy is not his stepmother's heir," she asserted rashly, forgetting, in her desire to defend Jeremy, that such information might not be public. "She must leave her fortune to her blood relations, the descendants of the princes of Sayn."

Leon raised an eyebrow in surprise, but he did not make the comment Marion was expecting to hear. He seemed lost in his own thoughts. The dog relaxed at his feet and the sunlight filtering through the trees fell on his darkly handsome face as he leaned back against the trunk of an evergreen. Everything about him seemed to belong to the forest, to the different shades of green, to the rays of sunlight falling on the path. He was the picture of strength and vigor and as unpredictable as the changing seasons.

Looking at him Marion found herself thinking that a woman in love with him would find him quite striking with his noble, albeit casual, attitude, his tanned face in the sunlight. Suddenly she recalled the flash of red, the red of a dress seen through a window the day she had come upon Leon's home in the middle of the forest. She couldn't resist the urge to question him.

"Tell me," she asked in as casual a tone as she could manage, "Do you know anything about a young woman by the name of Ida Somers?"

She had the impression that she had startled him, although he was doing a very good job of hiding it. He paused for a moment before answering.

"Yes," he said finally. "I know her quite well."

"She's very beautiful, isn't she?"

He agreed. "Very beautiful, indeed," he said with a smile. "Unfortunately, being beautiful is not always a good thing for a woman. Sometimes she may get carried away...and become the victim of her own beauty."

Impulsively Marion decided to persist. "I thought I saw her at your house the other day."

Leon did not deny it. "That's right. Ida was there," he replied. After a long pause he added, "Ida and I are friends."

"You must be, for her to come all the way into the forest to see you."

She had spoken more dryly than she had intended. It irritated her to hear him speak of friendship between himself and the beautiful young woman with the blond hair. Marion knew that he was lying, that there was something more intimate between them.

As though he felt the need to make some kind of explanation Leon continued. "She came to see me because she knows she can talk to me about her problems."

Now Marion was angry. "I must say that she gives every appearance of having a very serious problem."

Leon laughed bitterly. "She has," he said abruptly. "Very serious."

"But of course *you* don't have anything to do with it," she said caustically.

Leon looked at her with curiosity. He studied her face steadily for a moment before speaking.

"Yes, I think you could say that I do have something to do with it," he said sadly.

Marion was shocked—both by his honesty and his apparent lack of shame. She didn't want to know more. Everything Leon said upset her.

"I think I'll be going on my way," she murmured. Not

knowing how to handle the situation she turned abruptly and started walking up the path.

With relief she realized that Leon didn't try to catch up to her. At a bend in the path she ventured to look back. He was walking toward her, but slowly, having stopped to light a pipe. He didn't appear to be upset by her actions. Instead he seemed to be enjoying the walk, smoking his pipe, playing with his dog and generally enjoying the woods and wildlife around him.

I'll never understand that man, Marion thought angrily, wondering why he was continuing in her direction.

After a short distance, just around another sharp bend in the path, she came to a charming old wooden bridge over the stream. On the far side, set on a piece of land completely encircled by the stream, was a Japanese-style teahouse made of wood and supported by posts, which in some places were gently lapped by the water.

Marion was charmed. She wondered if Martha Koster was responsible for this quiet, secluded spot. She imagined Martha and Emile, the love of her life, coming here in the quiet of the evening. Marion climbed into the house and sat on the cushioned bench that extended around the entire circumference of the small building. A large hammock was strung across the end, looking out on the water. With surprise, Marion noted how deep and wide the stream had become, deep enough to dive into and to swim in. She looked upstream and found the explanation—a large stone dam had been built, creating a perfect swimming pond for hot summer days.

"It's a nice spot, isn't it," said a deep voice behind her, making her jump. "I guess I have to apologize again for frightening you," Leon said. "I assumed that you knew I was behind you."

"Of course," Marion said, blushing. "I forgot. Yes, it's lovely."

"If the water weren't so cold," Leon went on, "we could go in swimming." His eyes appraised her steadily. "I've already learned that you like the water."

Marion's pulse quickened. What did he mean? She wasn't sure. She was beginning to feel more than uneasy being alone with this man, so far from other people, in the middle of the forest. She shivered. It was cold in the shade of the teahouse. Again, she wished she had her other clothes. She felt almost naked under Leon's bold, masculine gaze.

"I like to come here on hot summer evenings," Leon continued. "I sleep here all night, in the hammock. The wildlife around here is used to solitude. It's like being one with them; they forget I am here."

Marion shivered. She imagined it would be beautiful here at night with the stars shining...but then she remembered the howls.

"But the wolves."

"The wolves don't bother me," Leon said simply.

Marion glanced up at him. He was standing, confident and strong, looking out at the water. She wondered how many times he and Ida had come to this spot—to swim, to stay the night, to....

As if reading her thoughts Leon turned to her. "I want to say something more to you. I said that it was true, that I do have something to do with Ida's 'problem'. But not in the way you think. I can't say anything more without hurting her, and I don't want to do that. She's really very upset and I'm concerned about her."

"I've had the feeling that she was terribly desperate," Marion said, relieved at last to be talking to *someone* about this, even if it was the person she suspected of being the cause of Ida's problem. "I know you might find this strange, but...."

"But what?"

Hesitantly, Marion went on.

"Is there anything I can do to help?"

"You?"

"Why not?" Marion asked quickly, somewhat surprised at this reaction. "There are times when only a woman can really help another woman. As a matter of fact I wanted very much to speak to her the other day."

Pensively, Leon looked at her delicate face, the silky hair, the soft gray eyes, and the words he spoke seemed totally unrelated to anything that had been said before.

"You don't have the strength to cope with the cruelties of this life."

He had moved a little closer to Marion and in his warm dark eyes, Marion could see kindness, perhaps even a touch of pity. She trembled and looked away. "It has nothing to do with me," she murmured. "We were talkng about Ida!"

He nodded his head. "Yes," he said sadly. "My advice to you," he continued in a harsh voice, "is that you'd be better off not bothering yourself about Ida. Besides," he added in the old sarcastic tone, "I'm sure Jeremy would forbid it."

He stopped talking for a moment. "In any case—" he paused, reaching out to stroke her bare shoulder in a comforting, tender way that sent a shock of pleasure through her body "—there's nothing you can do to cure her ills."

Now the only sound to be heard was the steady staccato rapping of a nearby woodpecker. Marion looked at Leon and for a moment it seemed that they were the only two people in the entire world. Then the doubts, the questions, came rushing back, disturbing the special quiet moment between them. What could have caused the rift between this man and Jeremy? And what was the nature of his close relationship to Ida? Did Ida love him?

Marion couldn't help but imagine that he would be an ardent, passionate lover. Quite the opposite, indeed, from Jeremy, who always seemed to be control of his emotions. How often had the young woman in the red dress rested her blond head against that broad chest? Had she listened to the beat of his heart, felt the comfort of his strong arms holding her close? Had she known his kiss?

The silence prolonged itself. The forest around them became strangely quiet. The moment seemed to take on a hidden meaning. The animal at rest at his master's feet suddenly twitched his ears, got to his feet and growled. Footsteps could be heard on the path and Marion turned to see her fiancé approaching.

"Jeremy!"

He had been the furthest thing from her mind and his sudden appearance surprised her.

"None other," he said, his tone sardonic.

He came closer, his hair as blond as Leon's was dark. But Jeremy's eyes were not on Marion. He was staring at Leon, who, in turn, was glaring at him. Dressed in his usual casual manner, his corduroy trousers hugging slim hips and his suede jacket slung over his wide shoulders, Leon seemed part of the woods, the sunlight, the stream. Jeremy, on the other hand, seemed somewhat out of place in his dark gray pinstripe suit. He turned to Marion. "I got your note," he explained, "and I've come to join you."

He put his hand on her shoulder in a gesture of possessiveness, but his eyes stared at Leon. A world of hate was encompassed by the look. A world in which Marion played no part. "It seemed to me, when I first saw you, that you were having a very serious conversation with...this man here."

The words he used were not characteristic of Jeremy. Usually he spoke very clearly, and certainly always sensibly. This time she was sure she had heard a tremor in his voice.

In a mocking tone Leon replied. "Apparently we can't hide anything from you." His dark eyes, which only a moment before had reflected warmth and kindness, now glittered with anger. "I'd wager you weren't too pleased by what you saw."

"No."

The exchange between the two men went over Marion's head. It was as if she weren't there at all, in spite of the fact that it was she who was at stake in this duel of words.

In the same mocking tone Leon continued. "Could it be that you're jealous? Are you afraid I might steal your fiancée, Jeremy? We all know that such things do happen, don't we?"

Marion saw Jeremy clench his fists as though he were making an effort to stop himself from striking out. The hatred between them seemed as vivid as the wind in the forest, the odor of the leaves on the trees, the noise of the woodpecker, the tense, watchful expression in the dog's eyes.

"If I ever..." growled Jeremy.

Leon raised his eyebrows and his lips curled in a sardonic smile. "If you ever what?"

There was no mistaking the challenge in his voice. The silence that followed was filled with almost unbearable tension. Then, as though giving way to some uncontrollable urge, Jeremy snarled, "I'm only going to tell you once, so listen. I don't want you bothering Marion."

"Was I bothering you?"

"No," Marion said, throwing an imploring look at Jeremy. "He wasn't, Jeremy—not at all."

"Well, let's just say that I'm not too happy about finding my future wife engaged in intimate conversation with a man not of her social status."

"What you really mean is that you consider me to be inferior, right?"

"Precisely!"

With an offensive arrogance Jeremy added, "You're nothing more than a simple employee of my mother's estate."

The manager glared at Jeremy and then suddenly started to laugh. Jeremy seemed stunned. With a shrug he took Marion by the arm and said, "Come on, let's get out of here."

It was quite obvious that he did not want to prolong the conversation. Marion turned to look back at Leon. The rays of the setting sun seemed to set his dark hair aflame.

"Good night," said Marion softly. She felt that she should apologize for Jeremy. Show somehow that she did not approve of his behavior, but she knew she could say nothing.

JEREMY AND MARION walked in silence for a while along the moss-covered path.

"Didn't you wear a jacket? And where are your shoes?

Why did you take them off?" Jeremy asked, an icy chill in his voice.

"It was hot... I thought I was alone, and I wanted to walk in the stream. They're up at the big boulder ahead."

"You are never alone, remember that."

They hiked briskly toward the boulder, Marion doing her best not to cry out in pain whenever she stepped on a sharp rock. In silence she put on her shoes and over-blouse. She felt better—suddenly it seemed very cold.

"Were you talking with Altamira for long?" Jeremy asked when she rejoined him.

"No. Just a few minutes."

In truth she couldn't really say how long they might have been talking. Time could have passed and she wouldn't have noticed.

"What were you talking about?"

"Oh, nothing in particular. Just this and that."

"Well, to tell you the truth, whatever the manager might choose to say really doesn't interest me. But I'm sure he must have tried to influence you... to twist things around."

"Twist things around? I don't know what you mean."

Jeremy seemed ill at ease and suddenly stopped on the path.

"Jeremy," asked Marion, looking up at him, "why were you so offensive with Leon?"

Jeremy pretended to be surprised. "Offensive? Me?"

"Yes. That's the only thing I can call it. And it was quite deliberate, too." She looked at him for a moment. "What is it between you and Leon?"

"Nothing. Nothing at all! What could there be? I simply dislike him. I detest his behavior. Besides, you remember this morning—seeing Ida in the park. Well... I just can't respect him for not helping her out."

Marion looked down. What Jeremy was saying was true. Yet there had been something in Leon's expression that made her wonder.

Marion looked at Jeremy, but she knew that she would find no clue in his clear eyes. She sighed, realizing all too well that Jeremy, like Leon, was not going to tell her anything at all about the reason for their mutual hatred. Trying to get information out of either of these two men was like banging her head against a wall.

"Do me a favor, will you?" Jeremy was saying. "Try to avoid any further contact with him." His voice gradually became calmer as he spoke. Then he looked at her with surprise. "Why are you trembling, darling?

Whenever he called her "darling" Marion had felt her heart fill with warmth. But this time the tender word, the caressing voice left her cold. Feeling a profound sadness come over her she sighed. "Oh, no reason," she said, shrugging her shoulders. "It's cold now."

Again they started to walk. At the end of the path the château rose austerely against the sky. In the rays of the setting sun scarlet geraniums nodded against the green grass of the lawn.

Marion was thinking that she should have been feeling a great joy, walking beside Jeremy beneath the tall trees. But somehow she felt very much alone. She thought about the man next to her, who was soon to be her husband, and realized that she scarcely knew him. There was no openness, no feeling of warm hearts meeting between them, none of those things that she had always imagined makes love profound and beautiful. But what did she know about love? She had been raised in an orphanage and then in foster homes. She had been told that she was lucky to have a warm bed to sleep in and food to eat—to ask for love was obviously asking for too much.

"That miserable Leon ruined what could have been a beautiful moment for us," Jeremy said, noticing Marion's troubled expression. "In fact he was almost the cause of our first quarrel. I will never allow that man—or anyone else, for that matter—to come between us."

He put his arms around her and kissed her. Pressed against hers, Jeremy's lips were firm and warm. For the first time, however, Marion felt nothing.

Chapter 9

When Marion and Jeremy walked into the living room of the château, Isabel greeted them with her favorite line. "Well, here come our two lovers!"

The wink of her eye and the sly smile that accompanied those words seemed somehow malicious.

"Did you enjoy your walk in the woods?" Mrs. Koster asked.

"It would have been very pleasant," replied Jeremy bitingly, "had I not come upon your manager having an intimate conversation with Marion."

Mrs. Koster made a gesture of annoyance with her hand. "Oh, Jeremy, let's not get into all that again! You know I like Leon and whatever you might have to say about him won't change anything."

"You just don't know him as I do!" Jeremy muttered.

"Well, he's worked for me for years. I should think that I know him well enough by now. Besides, there's just something about his personality I like. It's as simple as that. Your dislike for him is confusing. You didn't always feel this way. What happened?"

Jeremy scowled with displeasure. "Nothing happened. I just saw him for who he really was, that's all."

Isabel, strangely excited, started to talk about the

preparations for the wedding. Marion had designed her own wedding dress, a full-length white gown, which was being made at the shop where she had been working when she met Jeremy. She and Jeremy would be leaving for Paris in a few days to pick it up.

"Will you be gone long?" asked Mrs. Koster.

"Three or four days."

"Marion, I'm sorry, but..." Jeremy spoke with regret in his voice. "I won't be able to go with you. I have too many things to take care of here."

"But Jeremy..." Marion pleaded although she knew there was nothing she could do. She had been looking forward to their time away together. They had seen very little of each other since they arrived; Marion suspected that that was why they weren't as close as they had been before. If they could only get away by themselves for a few days—go out for an evening of dining and dancing as they had before they became engaged—then things could be better.

"Can't you go alone?" Jeremy asked. "You could still stay in the deluxe suite I had reserved in the Hilton. Maybe one of your friends could join you. It might be fun, darling. Do whatever you like—take your friends to dinner, to a play—the treat would be mine."

"Thank you, Jeremy, but if I'm by myself, I think I'd rather stay in my old place." Marion managed a smile somehow. "I'll go by myself. It will be okay. It's just that—" Marion paused. She didn't like talking about these things in front of Martha and Isabel. "It's just that I was really looking forward to spending some time with you," Marion said to Jeremy, completing her sentence.

"Well, this will make our trip to Italy all the nicer," Jeremy said. "That's one way of looking at it, darling."

After the wedding ceremony, they were to spend their honeymoon in Italy, in one of the lake regions. For Marion these preparations provided a more tangible form for her dream of happiness, which sometimes seemed to be slipping away from her.

The conversation about the wedding continued, Isabel

complaining that she had hoped it would have been a large regal affair, and expressing a doubt that Patricia, Marion's friend who was to be her maid of honor, would be well-versed on the necessary formalities.

Marion glanced at Martha and Jeremy, not daring to say anything. She was thankful that Marguerite and Beth had told her about Isabel's background, or she might now be feeling confused and angry. Nevertheless she was quite relieved when she could politely excuse herself to go to her room.

It took her a long time to fall asleep. The nightmare that plagued her rest was beginning to upset her more and more. An evening breeze billowed the ruffled organdy curtains, and in the surrounding mountains Marion heard the lonely howl of a wolf. She snuggled into her down comforter and pulled the fine embroidered silk sheets over her ears. She wondered what it might be like, alone with Leon, listening to the howl of the wolves. A shiver went through her entire body. The small fire in the ancient brick fireplace in her room was dying down. Now, the embers merely glowed and occasionally crackled.

Just before she fell into sleep she felt the familiar weight of Tiger settling at the foot of her bed. Even though the servants tried to keep Tiger away, he always found a way to get into her room. Marion dropped off to sleep with her hand against the cat's soft, silky fur, listening to his contented, throbbing purring. Just having him there was a comfort to her.

THE NEXT DAY, Marion went into town to do some last-minute shopping for her trip. On the way she asked the chauffeur to drop her off at Jeremy's office for a short time. She needed to see him, to speak to him. She had been thinking—she had something in mind that she thought might help.

Jeremy was at his desk when his secretary ushered her in. His blue wool suit was of the best material available in Europe, and the cut, which was very fashionable although tastefully conservative, complemented his trim and athletic build. His demeanor, his perfect features, his carefully groomed blond hair, made him the image of elegance, class and power. He seemed at home in this environment; authority came naturally to him and gave his features an animated expression that was not often there.

As Marion looked at him she felt proud that she would be marrying Jeremy Koster, that she would be his wife, although there were times when she felt too unsophisticated, too much an ordinary woman to keep up with him. Yet he had assured her that he wanted only her, just the way she was, that she shouldn't feel ill at ease meeting his friends and associates. Marion smiled thinking of the wonderful things he had told her during their evenings together in Paris, evenings filled with magic and promise and love. *Being loved by this man can only bring me joy*, she thought to herself.

"Lilian, hold all calls for me, will you? And tell Mr. Wilson to wait. I won't be long," Jeremy spoke into the intercom, smiling at Marion. "Well," he said, sitting back in his chair and putting his feet on his desk in an attitude of determined comfort, "what brings you here?"

"I was wondering if we could meet for lunch today. There's something I want to talk to you about."

"I'm sorry. I'm booked for lunch already. Why don't you say what you want to say now?"

Marion paused. It wasn't exactly the right atmosphere, but the way things had been going, this might be her only chance to talk to Jeremy alone.

"I want...I need to see more of you, Jeremy. In Paris, it was so nice. We talked and—"

"But that was holidays, darling, you can't expect me to always be available. I have work to do."

"I understand that, dear," Marion rushed on. "And that's what I want to talk to you about. Remember when we first met?"

"Of course."

"Well, remember how you came into the shop and

admired my sweater and we got to talking about how I had designed it and made it, and that you owned a knitting factory and wanted to take me to lunch to talk about my maybe working for you as a designer?" Marion's words tumbled out. "Do you remember?" she asked, stopping, her face flushed. *Why was she finding it so difficult to talk about this,* she wondered.

Jeremy simply nodded his head slowly, staring at her steadily.

"Well, I've been thinking about it. I'd *like* to do that. I know I'd be good at it. Maybe I'd have to take some courses, or be trained here, but I think I might be good at it and...and that way, we could see more of each other. We could work together, the way you had said."

Marion sat back in her chair, trying to relax. She had said all she had planned to say. She hadn't expected it to come out all at once as it did, or for it to be over so quickly. She waited for Jeremy to speak. He twisted in his chair and twirled a pen between his fingers. He was smiling. *Why isn't he saying anything,* Marion wondered.

"You funny little thing," he finally said with a laugh. "Don't you know that I was only saying all that just so you'd go out with me?"

Suddenly tears sprang to Marion's eyes. She felt humiliated, humbled and stupid. "You mean—"

"I thought you had forgotten about all that. Besides, dear, I want you at home. I'm sorry if you misunderstood," he added, noticing Marion's tears. "I thought you were so beautiful, I had to see you," he added in an attempt to comfort her. "Don't you see?"

His tone changed, became brisk and businesslike. "Darling, I can't stay with you any longer. Come, I'll walk you out."

Marion wiped her tears and stood. Jeremy took her elbow and guided her to the door. Outside he nodded briefly to a man Marion took to be Mr. Wilson and pushed her toward the door to the factory section outside the executive suite. "Where is Henry? Parked in front?"

Marion nodded. She still felt upset by their conversation. As they walked down the hall she looked around the factory at the workers who were busy operating the knitting machines.

"Are you interested in something in particular, Marion?" Jeremy asked.

"I was just looking for Ida, the woman we saw in the park yesterday."

Jeremy's eyes turned cold.

"Ida doesn't work here anymore," he said flatly. "Her work was not satisfactory and we had no choice but to fire her."

"Really!" Marion exclaimed. She was shocked. She had thought that Jeremy was sympathetic to the young woman's situation. She remembered his words the day she and Martha had found Ida crying in Jeremy's office. And she knew that a woman in Ida's condition could have a very hard time finding a job. It was certainly not going to help her.

"The poor woman. What is she going to do, Jeremy?"

"I don't know . . . and to tell you the truth, I don't care," Jeremy replied irritatedly. Then, more gently, he added, "You have to understand, my darling, that I run a factory. I can't concern myself with the fate of any one worker. If I did, there just wouldn't be any end to it."

"But, Jeremy—"

"No *buts*, Marion. I won't allow interference on business matters. You might as well get used to it."

Just as Marion was about to get into the car, Jeremy put his hand on her arm and said, "As soon as we get back from our honeymoon, you can learn to drive and then I'll buy you a car for your own personal use. That way you'll be able to get around as you please, instead of having to rely on the chauffeur."

"Oh, I'd like that," Marion said without emotion. She tried not to be upset. He was certainly as kind as he was handsome. How could she do anything but love him.?

WHEN SHE REACHED THE CENTER OF TOWN Marion shopped in a few of the boutiques. But wherever she went, whether it was in a shop or at the library, the attitude of people toward her seemed forced. The extent of their conversations with her was "Yes, miss," and "No, miss." As on the day before she felt that people were hiding behind their curtains watching her every move.

With relief, Marion realized that it was past noon. She would stop for a sandwich and a cup of coffee. Then at least she would feel free of the watching eyes that seemed to be following her everywhere.

She considered going into the little restaurant she and Martha had stopped in only a few days before. With a start Marion realized how little time had passed. It felt like months. The restaurant was crowded, however, and she would have to wait for a table. She decided to go to the less fancy coffee shop she had seen down the street.

The place was shabby, but clean. Plastic flowers graced the center of each formica table. With a tired sigh Marion slid into a booth, noticing with chargin that the cook and several of the customers had turned to stare at her. Should she go back to the little restaurant? Would it make any difference?

Why is everyone staring at me, she wondered. She was so unnerved that any second she was afraid she might break down and ask someone. Instead she stared at her menu, seeing nothing.

"What will you have?" a woman's distinctly chilled voice asked. Marion looked up. The woman looked pleasant enough. She was in her forties and had a round, motherly figure and worry lines around her face that told Marion that her life was not an easy one.

"Oh, a toasted tuna fish sandwich, please. And a cup of coffee. Thank you."

Without a word the woman turned. Just then a burly man in a grease-stained apron came through a steel-plated door that Marion guessed led to the kitchen. His face was flushed, and he looked angry.

Through the partly opened door, Marion heard a woman's voice, "Dad, wait!"

The handful of customers turned to look as a woman in red pushed her way through the door. She stopped dead in her tracks when she saw Marion seated at the far table. It was Ida.

The man looked at her and then turned to see why his daughter was so surprised. When he saw Marion, he went white. "You're not serving *her*, are you?" he exclaimed to the woman Marion guessed was his wife, taking the cup of coffee out of her hands.

Marion rose from her seat, tears in her eyes. She didn't want to stay where she wasn't welcome, but she desperately wanted to talk to Ida. Something told her that the young woman was at the center of the mystery that seemed to have plagued her since her arrival and, that Ida very badly needed help. Marion felt torn inside by the expression of hurt and desperation she saw in the other woman's eyes. She seemed like a frail animal caught in a trap, with no hope of escape.

Marion took a step toward Ida. She was determined to reach out to her, but throwing Marion a look of mingled fear and longing, she bolted from the room.

With sad resignation, Marion slipped on her coat and went outside. There was no sense in staying in town any longer. She felt alienated, unwanted, and she didn't know why. Her days, like her nights, were beginning to feel like a nightmare. Her heaven like hell.

The chauffeur was waiting patiently in the car for her, reading a local newspaper. "Good day, miss," he said cheerfully. "How was your morning?"

"Oh...okay I guess," Marion replied listlessly. For a moment she thought about asking Henry what might be going on, but she felt foolish and she was afraid that he would tell others, so she decided against it.

She didn't know whom she could talk to. She thought of confiding in Martha, but she was afraid of upsetting her; Marion knew how susceptible Martha's health was to emotional upset. At all costs, she must not be disturbed.

For a second she thought of talking to Leon, but immediately banished the thought from her mind. Something about him disturbed her deeply. And she found that she was easily upset by whatever he said. It would be better to avoid even the chance of running into him.

"Henry, do we have to return through the woods? Is there another way?"

"Yes, I could go the back route. It's longer, but it's pretty, too. Do you want me to go that way?"

"Yes, thank you," she sighed. She didn't want to risk running into Leon. She had had such an upsetting day she only wanted to go back to her room and rest. If she didn't she felt she would fall to pieces, and tomorrow she would be leaving for Paris. It wouldn't do to arrive in such a terrible state.

The sleek Mercedes pulled to stop in the grand curved driveway in front of the entrance to the château. As Marion bent over to gather her parcels, her door was opened for her.

"May I help, Marion?" asked a deep voice she instantly recognized. *Leon.*

Marion started to tremble and her heart was beating very fast. "No, thank you anyway, Leon," she replied, glancing very briefly into his penetrating eyes. Her heart jumping, she looked quickly away. She had wanted to avoid meeting him. Just seeing him like this was so disturbing.

"I suppose you'll be getting into trouble if you talk to me," he said caustically after the chauffeur had gone with the car. "At least let me help you in with your parcels. That shouldn't be against the rules."

"Please, Leon. Don't talk like that," Marion pleaded softly. He sounded so cold and hurtful, she couldn't stand it any longer. "Jeremy wasn't very polite to you yesterday, I know that. He was simply annoyed to find us talking to each other. Can't you forgive him? Surely you can understand."

"It's not important, really. We're used to each other. Our conversations usually are anything but pleasant. Besides, I'm more concerned about you. For a woman about to be married to the man she loves, you seem quite unhappy."

Tears came to Marion's eyes for the third time that day. "Why are you talking to me like this?" she asked. "What have I ever done to you?"

Leon's rugged features softened and the warm expression Marion had seen the day before now appeared in his dark eyes. "You haven't done anything to me...but enchant me," he said softly, a beguiling grin on his face.

"Please, don't say things like that," Marion protested, her heart fluttering alarmingly.

"But you have! But then—I'm sure I'm only one of many men who have come under your spell, Marion," Leon added in a whisper. "But knowing Jeremy as I do, I wonder how he can appreciate such a treasure."

He was talking with such incredible audacity that Marion couldn't believe what she was hearing. She covered her ears with her hands and cried, "How would you know! I don't want to hear any more of this. I can't take any more of your sarcasm and your mean insinuations."

She loved Jeremy and he loved her. Of that she was sure. He had no reason to marry her unless he loved her. Why was Leon tormenting her, trying to cause trouble and doubt? She didn't want to know. She simply wanted him to go away.

"You'd like to think you could break us up," she said in a faltering voice, "but you'll never succeed. I don't know why, but you're trying to hurt Jeremy. Are you trying to hurt him through me? Is that your scheme? You've already ruined the life of one woman I can think of. How many others are there?"

Marion paused for breath. She was shaking and tears were flowing down her cheeks. "I love Jeremy and I'm going to marry him. In less than two weeks he'll be my husband. Why are you trying to destroy my happiness?"

Her joy, in fact, was wavering like a candle's flame in

the wind. Regaining her composure she said, "What business is it of yours, anyway? Don't you have a life of your own to live? Have you no love of your own to worry about?"

The deathly white face of Ida in the restaurant that day came to her mind. She could see the pale face, and the hunted eyes—expressing both a need for help and fear. Why? Out of some absurd feeling of spite, some desperate rebellion, Marion said, "The truth is—you're jealous. You envy Jeremy."

"I'm sorry that you have such a low opinion of me, Marion."

He looked at her gravely for a moment, his eyes seeming to penetrate her very soul. Once more, the light from the setting sun seemed to be setting his hair aflame. From somewhere among the branches of a nearby tree pure treble notes of birdsong cascaded through the golden air.

"Love is a unique feeling," said Leon slowly, "singular and quite extraordinary. To most it comes but once in a lifetime. I once imagined—I don't know why—that despite all the things you have said, your heart was not entirely enthusiastic."

A bitter smile, touched with disdain, hovered on his lips. "It has never been my intention to hurt you. I won't say anything more about Jeremy since it displeases you."

"But it won't change the way you think," she sighed.

"My thoughts and feelings are between myself and my God," he said abruptly. "Good night, Marion."

He nodded his head, turned around and walked away. With an effort Marion pulled herself together and ran up the steps to the château. She suddenly hated this man who seemed to have the ability to make her doubt her own happiness, to spoil her dream, even her love for Jeremy. She wished she had never met him, never known the warmth of his dark eyes, never seen the strength of his arms, the tender curve of his smile.

Chapter 10

Paris is quite pleasant at this time of the year, Marion thought as
she came out of the train station. Of course there was
none of the fresh greenery of the Vosges, nor the dark
blue of the mountainous horizon. There wasn't the rich
beauty of the evergreens, or the variety of scents and
sounds of the magnificent forest. However, there were
other manifestations of beauty, albeit of a very different
kind, that could be found nowhere but in the city.

She had decided to refuse Jeremy's offer of a room at
the Hilton. She yearned for the familiar, and so it was
with relief that she climbed the stairs to her old room.
She had kept the room where she had been living all the
time she had been working. . . a time that seemed so long
ago, and yet in fact only a week had passed. Compared to
her room at Grunberg, this one seemed very small, and
because she had been away, her few possessions, which
had once been so familiar to her, now seemed foreign.
Marion put down her suitcase and opened the window,
leaning out to look down onto the street.

It was the everyday Paris, so often missed by tourists.
Women walked slowly, followed by the eyes of men. A
flower girl offered roses to the passersby. Marion closed

the window, shaking her head. There would be no escape from her feeling of uneasiness here. What illusion had led her to believe that she could recapture her early enchantment with Jeremy by coming back? Where, indeed, would she ever be able to find it?

She washed her face and combed her hair and then went out into the street. A man passing by whispered a compliment and the flower girl offered her a rose. When she entered the shop where she used to work exclamations greeted her from every direction.

"You've finally come back! What on earth have you been doing with yourself?"

"I've been wondering if you'd forgotten your promise to have me as your maid of honor," said Patricia.

Patricia was one of the most beautiful young women in Paris, one of the most sought-after models in the industry. Seeing her own reflection in the mirror alongside these women so carefully made up because of their profession as models, Marion considered herself to be pale and abysmally plain. And then she remembered what someone up there at the château had said to her, a man who was not the one she would be spending the rest of her life with. She tried to recall the compliments paid to her by Jeremy, but any that came to mind seemed dull and very conventional.

"Tell us," her friends were asking, "what's it like? Is the château really huge?

"Enormous. Thirty rooms, at least. The wing where Jeremy and I will be living has been almost completely renovated now."

"And what about your incredible Jeremy? Is he as handsome as ever?"

"Well, yes...I think so!"

"Of course, he came to Paris with you, didn't he?"

"No. He had to stay there to settle some work matters."

"It must have been something pretty important," Natalie said with a frown, "for him to let you come to Paris alone." It was quite outside Natalie's understand-

ing that anything to do with business could be important
enough to interfere with matters of the heart.

"I suppose," replied Marion. "I really have very little to
do with what goes on at the factory."

With a strange ache in her heart Marion had to admit
that she really felt that nothing should have been important enough to keep Jeremy from coming to Paris with
her.

"Tell us about your future mother-in-law. Do you like
her? Is she nice to you?"

This was something Marion was able to talk about
with complete ease. "More than nice," she replied. "She
is very warm and affectionate, not at all like the
mothers-in-law people are forever making jokes about,
if you know what I mean."

The owner of the shop appeared. Carmen was one of
those women whose age would always remain a mystery, whose eyes suggested that she had seen many
different sides of life, and whose almost-perfect figure
could only be the result of years of severe dieting. Marion's rings immediately caught her attention. "What
incredible jewels!" she exclaimed.

Marion held out her hand. On her ring finger was
Jeremy's diamond; the emerald given to her by her
future mother-in-law sparked on her middle finger.
"Mrs. Koster gave me the emerald," she said. "It's a
family heirloom and is supposed to guarantee good
luck."

"Well, my dear, it certainly looks as though you've
made it big!" said Carmen

"But are *you* feeling okay? Somehow you don't look
very good," declared Natalie.

In her own mind Marion had to agree. It was beginning to plague her. She didn't feel the way a woman who
is to be married very soon should feel. Something in her
heart was unfulfilled. There was a kind of uncertainty in
the way she felt, and she had to admit to herself she was
not entirely happy.

To hide her true feelings she started to laugh and talk

with a nervous kind of animation. "The countryside is so beautiful," she said. "And then there's the forest ...."

She stopped. Mention of the forest recalled the picture of a man with dark red hair and warm expressive eyes. She shouldn't even be thinking about him, but somehow, she couldn't forget him.

"Look, Marion!" Patricia called out, interrupting Marion's thoughts. She came into the room holding the wedding dress that Marion had designed for herself.

Marion gasped, and shook her head with pleasure. It was even more beautiful than she had imagined.

Before they had left Paris, Jeremy had insisted—to her pleasure, of course—that she have a complete wardrobe made for herself. She would be leading a new life, and the clothes she owned were inappropriate. They had spent hours poring over fashion magazines and he had gone with her when she had tried on suits and dresses and even casual clothes in innumerable high-fashion shops. Many of the things Jeremy had chosen were being made for her here—in the shop where she had once worked. After years of having admired the fine fabrics and exquisite fashion and detailing, she felt like a child let loose in a candy factory having so many exquisite outfits made for her. Although many were more sophisticated than she would have liked, she imagined she would get used to them with time. And, anyway, what mattered was that Jeremy liked the way she looked.

But the wedding dress—this she had insisted on designing herself. It was going to be a surprise. She knew Jeremy was skeptical, but she had held firm. And now...now that she saw it, she was glad. It was a dress she would treasure forever.

"Please, put it on!" Patricia urged. "We've all been so excited about it, we can hardly stand it."

Marion smiled and allowed herself to be shepherded into the back room. She took off her clothes and slipped the delicate gown over her head, the layers of finely stitched pearl-white silk floating around her like a cloud. The fine layers had been gathered into the fitted bodice in a flattering and womanly curve. In the dress Marion had the breathtaking beauty of an innocent girl on the threshold of becoming a woman. Tiny pearls edged the deep, round neckline, which emphasized the graceful, slender line of Marion's neck and shoulders. Slender sleeves were gathered into a wisp of a cuff buttoned with a pearl, apparently modest, but offering tantalizing glimpses of smooth fair skin through carefully worked openings in the gathers.

"Marion, you look like an angel."

"Like you're from heaven. Oh, you look so beautiful I think I'm going to cry," Carmen said. "Have you ever thought of becoming a designer, Marion...seriously?"

Marion blushed with confusion. She remembered all too clearly her painful conversation with Jeremy the day before. "Don't be silly, Carmen."

"I'm serious. That dress is as good as any famous designer's. If you don't mind I'd like to put it in the window. After you're married, of course, and for only a week or so—or whatever you want. If you agree, that is."

"In the window? Really?" That was quite an honor. This was one of the most fashionable shops in Paris. She couldn't believe it. "Of course, I'm flattered, Carmen."

"And would you mind if I send a photograph of it to some of the magazines and newspapers? I would name you as the designer, of course."

"Yes...yes," Marion murmured, dazed from the unexpected turn of events.

She turned full circle in front of the mirror, the layers of fine silk "whispering" to her as she moved. Wistfully, her hand reached for a spot near her left shoulder where a tiny, delicate birthmark in the shape of a four-leaf clover was nestled. *My good-luck mark,* she had always called it. She had debated whether or not to design the dress to cover the mark. It was pretty, in its own way. She liked it and she had decided to let it show, even though Jeremy had asked her to design a closed-neck bodice. Looking at her reflection in the mirror, she knew

she had made the right decision, and she felt that Jeremy
would think so, too. She would buy shoes and jewelry to
go with the dress and then all would be complete.

"The veil!" Carmen exclaimed, rushing into the back
of the shop. "We are so overwhelmed by this young
beauty that we have forgotten her veil."

Marion laughed and gasped again as Carmen and two
others returned, bearing a delicate heap of silk lace so
fine that it seemed spun from cobwebs. Carefully, Carmen positioned the veil on Marion's head.

It suited her fragile and whimsical beauty perfectly,
framing her delicate features and the fine wisps of curls
that were always working their way out of place.

"Now you'll have to tell Jeremy to be careful with
this—no violent, passionate kisses at the altar. Not until
later, of course."

"Carmen, I love it. I can't believe the beautiful job
you've done. I think I'll marry the dress," Marion joked,
the sparkle coming back to her eyes.

"Oh, dear," the seasoned lady sighed. "Don't
tell Jeremy. I don't want any jealous lovers hanging
around...especially over a dress."

And then it was time to try on the dresses and suits
that were to be her trousseau. There was also the matter
of Patricia trying on her dress.

The seamstress who was to make a few minor adjust-
ments to all her clothes remarked, "You've lost a little
weight, Marion. I'll have to take everything in."

Marion tried on all her dresses and a suit of the shade
of blue that is almost gray that she was to wear on her
wedding day to travel to Italy. For a while it was fun, just
seeing herself in so many different outfits. But when the
excitement was over, she found herself heavyhearted.
Something was making her feel unhappy and oppressed.

Finally, when Marion and Patricia were alone, Patricia
asked her what was wrong.

"Why, nothing. Everything is fine."

She pretended to be surprised at the question, but her
friend was not fooled.

"Except for a few moments when you were trying on your wedding dress, you didn't seem happy. In fact I'd be willing to swear you're not. Your eyes are sad and you seem uncertain, somehow, as though you're questioning the future. To tell you the truth, your eyes are *full* of questions."

"You're just imagining things, Patricia. I am happy...really I am."

"I wonder."

"Please, Patricia."

Marion couldn't admit that all those questions were about herself. Nor could she say that she didn't want to dwell on the questions for fear that she might discover some of the answers. "Please, let's not talk about me all the time," Marion pleaded, yearning to change the subject. "Can you have dinner with me tonight? Jeremy insisted that I take you to dinner—to the Ritz he said, but we can go wherever you like."

"You're kidding! The Ritz? That will cost a small fortune. Oh, God! What will I wear? Are you sure, Marion?"

"Absolutely," Marion beamed as Patricia gave her a big bear hug, and for a while the two women chattered and gossiped with their usual animation.

It's such a comfort to be with friends, Marion thought sadly as she left the shop. *What's the matter with me, anyway*, she asked herself as she joined with the late-afternoon crowd on the street. *Am I sick?*

She would have liked to have been able to believe that the way she looked was because of some physical ailment. Why else would she be feeling so dreadful? What else could be making her feel so unhappy? After all, she was to marry the man of her dreams in a few days...wasn't she?

Chapter 11

When Marion's train finally arrived at the station near Grunberg, the sky was overcast with heavy dark clouds. Swallows fluttered overhead. Jeremy was not at the station to meet her as she had hoped he would be. Instead Henry, Mrs. Koster's chauffeur, was waiting for her. With great care Marion put the boxes containing her wedding dress and all her other new clothes into the car and settled back into the comfortable seat. Soon Henry was drawing up before the great front door of the château. She did not have time to be surprised that none of the family was there to greet her. Having heard the car, the maid Jeanne appeared, breathless with excitement.

"Is *madam* all right?" Marion asked, becoming worried.

"Quite well," replied the maid, "considering the shock she's just had and all the things that have been going on around here."

Astounded, Marion looked at the girl. "What shock? What's been happening?"

"Oh—you don't know?"

"Of course not? How could I?"

"Haven't you seen the newspapers? There's certainly been enough printed about it."

"Jeanne! Tell me what's been happening!" There was a sinking feeling in Marion's heart. "Well, are you going to tell me?"

In her excitement Jeanne could hardly find the words to explain. "Miss Ida was found dead...drowned."

"Ida! Drowned?"

"Yes...in the Green Pond."

The two women looked at each other in stunned silence for a moment.

"At first it was thought to be an accident," Jeanne finally went on. "But then the police reported that they had discovered evidence that it was murder—that she had been strangled."

"Murder! Are you sure?"

"Yes. And Leon Altamira has been arrested."

"Leon?"

"Yes. You know, he and Ida were...uh, very close friends. At one time there was even talk that they might get married. And then she got into trouble." The maid looked away. "It seems they had a terrible fight...possibly over another man."

The words struck Marion like a physical blow. Her heart felt as if it had just been drained of all its blood.

"But, Jeanne...are you quite sure?"

"Very sure, *mademoiselle*. The police arrested Leon this morning."

Even though she hadn't been paying much attention to Tiger, who was rubbing against her legs affectionately, Marion suddenly bent down and picked up the cat, holding his comforting warmth against her chest where he purred contentedly.

"Now, there's one that really missed you," Jeanne went on. "I did everything I could to keep him out of your room, but he always found a way to get in."

As they stepped into the hallway Isabel appeared out of nowhere and cut into the conversation. "So—there's one more tragedy at Grunberg! Mind you, I never did like that Leon Altamira and I never tried to hide the way I felt about him from Martha. I've told her all along just how I felt."

There was an odious touch of triumph in her voice. "When Martha heard what had happened, of course she went into shock," she added, shrugging her bony shoulders. "She keeps insisting there must be some mistake and that Leon will soon be released. You know how she is. Martha has never been able to admit being wrong."

"It was bound to happen," muttered Jeanne, somewhat enigmatically. "I mean. . .Ida. She was always so easily abused."

"Jeremy couldn't pick you up at the train station," said Isabel abruptly. "This whole affair has caused quite a stir around here, particularly because Ida used to be employed at the factory. The police have been here several times to see Jeremy today."

Without answering, Marion simply nodded her head. She looked at the boxes containing her wedding dress and trousseau. What did any of it matter? What importance could all of this have now? Leon had been accused of murdering that beautiful young woman.

There was a prolonged and awkward silence. Marion took a few shaky steps before stopping to lean against a table. The words that were being said were like the stab of a dagger, and they conjured unbearable images in her mind. Leon Altamira arrested for murder! That man, so obviously meant for a life of freedom. How could he survive in a prison cell? The whole thing was unbelievable.

What of his faithful companion, the large black dog he called Satan? Marion didn't dare ask; both women seemed to be looking at her with suspicion.

"Aren't you feeling well, Marion?" Isabel asked.

"No. . .not very," Marion replied. Feeling the need to add something else she said, "The trip must have tired me. And then there's the weather. It's so hot."

Something weak and weary in her voice made the explanation quite plausible.

"Yes," agreed Isabel. "It feels like we're going to have

a storm. How was Paris?" she asked in a distant and brittle voice.

Marion managed some kind of an answer and soon the conversation turned to a discussion of her trip. "I'll have to ask you to excuse me," she said finally. "I must go upstairs and change. Perhaps I'll feel a little better later."

Slowly she climbed the stairs to her room, but she did not find the solitude she was seeking. Jeanne, the servant with the bold inquisitive eyes, had followed her, bearing the boxes of clothes. She lifted the dresses from their soft tissue wrappings and carried them to the closet. Curious to know the latest Parisian fashions, she made ecstatic remarks and asked all kinds of questions. Desperate to escape, Marion went into the bathroom and washed her hands mechanically. She felt like a sleepwalker; she was deeply shocked by the news. She needed to rest, to think.

Returning to her room, Marion stood for a moment and looked at the young woman who was carefully putting away the dresses. "Jeanne...?"

The maid stopped in mid movement, a hanger in her hand. "Yes, *mademoiselle?*"

Marion hesitated for a second, then asked the question feverishly burning in her mind. "Do you know what Ida was wearing when her body was taken from the pond?"

The image she had of the lovely blond woman was almost too powerful for her to handle. But the memory of the look of desperation on the young woman's face haunted her. She had only ever seen her wearing a red dress and that was the way she would always remember her. "Was Ida wearing a red dress when she drowned in the Green Pond?"

Marion pictured the unfortunate woman, the red dress draping her body like a scarlet shroud, soiled and muddied from the murky water. In one of those incongruous detours of the mind her imagination had become obsessed by this single detail.

Jeanne raised her eyebrows, obviously perplexed by the question. "I really don't know." Then, her eyes lighted up. "I know she often wore a bright red dress, though. It must have cost quite a lot of money. Certainly more than she'd be able to afford on the salary she was making," she added maliciously.

Since Marion didn't seem inclined to say anything more Jeanne went back to hanging up the dresses. Watching her moving back and forth, Marion could feel exhaustion gradually getting the best of her. "You may go now, Jeanne," she said. "My headache seems to be getting worse. I'll take some aspirin and try to get a little rest before dinner."

She knew very well that she would not be able to rest, that she would not be able to stop the questions rushing through her mind, but she needed to be alone and any excuse would do.

"Very well," Jeanne said. Annoyed at having been dismissed when she was so anxious to talk, she closed the closet door with a snap and walked out of the room.

Finally, Marion was alone, but unable to lie down or even sit still in a chair, she paced back and forth across the room, like a prisoner in a cell. Stretched out on his favorite spot at the foot of the bed, Tiger watched with his enigmatic golden eyes.

Her head was full of images and ideas and yet she was unable to make sense out of them. They hovered oppressively, fraught with danger . . . as ominous as the heavy clouds of a summer storm. She felt confused. She couldn't make out what her feelings were. Try as she might she simply couldn't put a name to what she was feeling. The only thing that emerged clearly was a sense of despair.

Leon and Ida were lovers. Or, at least, they had been. It didn't surprise her. She had as much as known this for a long time. But why did she feel so dreadful now that she was positive about it?

And then, according to Jeanne, Ida had left Leon for someone else. Marion did not ask herself who that "someone else" might be. She wasn't interested. All that interested her was the man with the dark red hair and piercing eyes. From the depths of her troubled heart, from the maelstrom of ideas bombarding her, one question emerged. *Leon, could you have loved that beautiful girl so much that you couldn't bear to lose her? Could you have preferred to see her dead, rather than belong to someone else?*

The thought seared like a brand in her mind.

And yet she simply couldn't convince herself that the manager was guilty of murder. She couldn't picture such a proud and arrogant man strangling a defenseless woman, then dumping her body in a pond to make it look as if she had drowned. He had spoken with such caring, such sincere feeling about Ida's plight. She could see the virile face beneath the short curly hair, the wide, generous mouth, the eyes that had looked at her with such tenderness and warmth. No, a man with such eyes could not be guilty of murder! Marion tried to recall each one of their conversations, so few, and yet so charged with emotion. She tried to weigh each word in an effort to discover the essence of the man, as if this were more important than anything else. It was not just a question of words, voice, looks. More important were the hidden meanings, the very things that were left unsaid.

Marion would occasionally stop pacing to look out the window, lifting her eyes to the darkening sky. Oh how she regretted not having spoken to Ida, when it seemed as if that was what the desperate woman had wanted most of all. Now Marion was angry with herself for not answering the silent cry for help she had sensed so clearly.

Yes, she should have approached Ida. But then, what would the result have been? She would never know. Now, Ida was dead. Beyond reach. The lovely blond Ida would be silent forever and so would the life she carried within her. Now, Marion would never know what it was she wanted to tell her, and a small voice kept needling her conscience. *Perhaps*, it said, *you could have helped. Perhaps, you could have saved Ida's life.*

MARION SHUDDERED when she heard the dinner bell. She was finding it very difficult to bring her mind back to the present. Like a zombie she went to the bathroom and freshened up. She would have preferred to remain in her room alone, but she could find no reason to do so. Furthermore she had no wish to insult Mrs. Koster by not appearing for dinner the night of her return from Paris. Reluctantly she made her way downstairs where Jeremy was waiting for her.

As soon as she walked into the room, he jumped to his feet and came to her. "My darling!" he said. "I'm so happy to see you."

He was, as always, impeccably dressed. His navy suit was tailored to fit him perfectly. But, in the late afternoon light still coming through the window, he seemed a little older. New lines seemed to have appeared on his forehead and at the corners of his eyes the tiny crows-feet had become more pronounced. It was as if the beautiful archangel was becoming mortal.

Jeremy hugged her, seeming not to notice that his fiancé's lips were avoiding his. "Forgive me for not picking you up at the station as I had intended to do," he said, "but so many things seemed to be happening at once. My schedule was nothing but chaos."

He was speaking quietly as usual, but Marion felt that he was forcing himself to be calm. "I believe you already know what has happened?"

"Yes," replied Marion in a voice that seemed to echo strangely in the room. "I am aware."

He ran his fingers through his hair and sighed. "A most unpleasant affair."

"Poor Ida!"

Jeremy turned his head. "Yes...poor Ida," he repeated. Mrs. Koster and Isabel came into the room. Mrs. Koster hugged Marion affectionately and asked her if she had had a good trip. She lowered herself into a chair with a sigh; she seemed very tired.

A pall of sadness seemed to be hanging over the château. Only Isabel seemed touched. Her eyes, normally clouded with anxiety, now sparkled with excitement. Mrs. Koster asked Marion a few questions about her stay in Paris, but it was evident that her mind was elsewhere. Before long she began to speak of what was bothering her. "You've heard about what happened while you were away?" she asked.

"Yes," Marion replied. "I've been informed...and I must say, the whole affair makes me very sad. I knew Ida only by sight, but she was quite beautiful. What a horrible thing to die so young and in such a dreadful way."

Unable to say any more, she stopped.

"Ida got just what she deserved," Isabel interrupted viciously. "There are far too many girls of her type in this world."

Unpleasant at the best of times, Isabel's voice now became shrill. Marion had to stop herself from covering her ears with her hands.

"It doesn't surprise me at all that she had come to a tragic end. She was the kind of woman who invites tragedy...as a lightning rod attracts lightning."

Mrs. Koster shook her head. "Well, maybe she was too beautiful for her own good," she said. "But to die such a death is atrocious! And no one except Marion seems to have had a word of pity for the poor woman."

"You're mistaken, mother," said Jeremy. "Ida's death has affected me very much." His voice, though smoothly controlled, held a strange undercurrent. He seemed, in fact, to be feeling sincere regret at the death of his employee. Perhaps he was sorry, now, that he had been so harsh with her.

"At any rate," said Mrs. Koster, "it was absolutely ridiculous for the police to have arrested Leon." She paused and looked around the room before continuing. "He couldn't possibly have had anything to do with this crime," she concluded finally.

"He has been released," Jeremy said dryly, seeming less than pleased about this latest development.

Marion sighed but said nothing. She was relieved to hear that Leon was free, but she couldn't shake the uneasy feeling that persisted no matter how hard she tried to ignore it.

"I don't believe it!" exclaimed Isabel.

"Well, it's true, whether you believe it or not," Jeremy replied. "There wasn't sufficient evidence to hold him in custody any longer."

"I never thought he'd be held for very long," Mrs. Koster said. "The charge was completely without grounds from the very beginning."

"He's not out of the woods yet!" Jeremy shot back. "There's some very strong evidence against him. There's ample proof, for instance, that there was a relationship between him and Ida, a relationship that Ida broke off, apparently only recently."

"Can we be sure about that?"

"Altamira himself admitted it."

"So?" she shot back.

"So it could have affected your precious manager in any number of different ways. Jealousy does strange things to people, you know. He could have lost his head and acted irrationally. It certainly wouldn't be the first crime of passion this world has ever known."

Marion listened in silence, trying not to move. She was afraid that if she said one word, moved even slightly, the strange feeling inside of her would surface, and it was a feeling she did not want to rouse.

"You're talking nonsense," Mrs. Koster said flatly. "I know enough about men to be very sure that Leon is not the sort who would seek vengeance against a woman because she betrayed him. He might hate...but he would never kill. He would simply stop loving her, that's all."

The words were a great consolation to Marion. They were an expression of her own hopes, her belief in what she considered to be the truth.

Isabel seemed surprised and very annoyed. "But he was the only logical choice," she said. "Where will the police look for the guilty one now?"

"There's nothing to say, yet, that he isn't guilty,"

Jeremy snapped. "They only need proof, that's all."
Nervously he walked to the window and looked outside. The sun was setting, lighting the sky with beautiful shades of red and gold. For centuries this forest had
been the site of countless dramas, some known, some
not, some punished, some not.

"Perhaps they should be looking for Ida's last lover,"
said Mrs. Koster. "No one seems to be thinking of him
as a possible suspect."

Isabel opened her mouth to say something, but
changed her mind, and Jeremy quickly turned around.

"The mayor is related to Ida's family. Surely he must
be aware of who Ida was going out with," Mrs. Koster
said. "And it seems a bit strange that Isabel and you,
Jeremy, seem so eager to hang Leon. You've always
hated him and now I suppose you see an opportunity to
quench your thirst for revenge." She was angry. After
a pause she went on, her tone very severe. "You really
disappoint me, Jeremy . . . and you, too, Isabel. Despite
the many years we've been living together, I suddenly
have the feeling that I don't know you at all."

"Come, come, now, Martha—"

Isabel interrupted on a whining note, "I didn't mean
to be unkind—I was just repeating what I heard."

"That will be enough!" said Mrs. Koster dryly. "And
don't start blubbering! I can't stand it"

There was a moment of silence. The sun had gone
down and in the dim light of dusk, disquieting shadows
formed in the forest and on the pathways. An ominous
feeling seemed to pervade everything and from time to
time a flash of lightning signaled the coming of the first
storm of summer.

Jeremy rubbed his face with his hand, as though he
wished to erase the traces of exhaustion that suddenly
had appeared. "Isn't there anything else we can talk
about?" he asked. "This is getting a little morbid."

He looked at Marion with a forced smile. "Just
imagine, Marion. In a few days we'll be getting
married."

Mrs. Koster wasn't listening. "That pond," she murmured. "There's something positively evil about it."

Marion understood now that this latest tragedy at the Green Pond had recalled the one of many years before, when Mrs. Koster's granddaughter had drowned. During the last few moments Mrs. Koster seemed to be showing signs of extreme fatigue. Her face was pale, her nostrils pinched. The early indications of cardiac problems. Marion knew that Martha had a heart condition and took medication to control it. She never went anywhere without it.

"My pills," sighed Mrs. Koster. "In the dining room...on the mantelpiece. Quick. Quick!"

Jeremy and Marion ran to the dining room, but Isabel, who was closest to the doorway, was the first to reach the small bottle of medication. She rushed back to Mrs. Koster and handed her a pill and a glass of water from a nearby tray. As Marion anxiously watched, she noticed that Isabel's eyes held a curiously speculative light.

Chapter 12

In spite of Mrs. Koster's obvious indisposition the meal was served and eaten as if nothing had happened. There was no further mention of the tragedy, nor were the names of Ida or Leon heard for the remainder of the evening. However the shadow of the beautiful young woman in the red dress seemed to hover in the dark corners of the room. It was a chilling thought that Ida had violently, forcefully, lost her life not far from the château where they were now quietly eating as they would on any other evening.

Marion couldn't help but imagine the cold, murky scene, and a haunting image of the young woman's helpless struggle when she knew her life was at risk kept recurring in Marion's mind. What had really happened? Had Ida begged? Wept? Had she fought or screamed? And who in this small, familiar villiage could have murdered her...and why? Could it have been Leon? Was Leon's passionate nature such that it could turn to a ruthless, inhuman urge to take another's life as easily as it turned to tenderness...and love? Marion didn't know, but the questions and thoughts sickened her. Try as she might she found it difficult to eat...or to talk.

In a somewhat weary voice Mrs. Koster, always a gracious hostess, was trying to keep the conversation going. Jeremy was doing what he could to help her along, all the while continuing to act out his role as a concerned and attentive fiancé toward Marion, who sat beside him.

"Are you all right, Marion?" he asked.

"Yes—I'm fine. I'm still tired from my trip, that's all."

"How was your trip?" Mrs. Koster asked. "Were you able to find everything you needed?"

"Yes. And I was very pleased with the work Carmen did, as well."

"Carmen?"

"The woman I used to work for."

"Are you keeping these gowns a secret, my dear?" Martha asked, her voice revealing a hint of exhaustion. "Or can I see them...tomorrow, perhaps?"

"Of course, I'd love to show them to you. But," she said, stopping to smile at Jeremy, "the wedding dress will be a secret until next Saturday."

"When is your friend Patricia coming?"

"Thursday evening. That way she will be here for the rehearsal."

"It's a pity that this tragic incident came up just before your wedding," Mrs. Koster noted sadly. "Perhaps you should—"

"No," Jeremy interrupted. "I know what you are going to say and it's wrong. The wedding will proceed no matter what."

"I certainly agree," Isabel burst in. "You can't let riffraff change your life. After all—"

"Isabel! All right—it was only a suggestion. Well, don't forget then: a small luncheon party for you both tomorrow afternoon. My friend, Mrs. Martineau— you remember her, don't you, Marion? Well, she'll be coming and I've invited the Reverend Mr. Lenôtre, too, so perhaps you will have a chance to work out any last-minute details with him."

Mrs. Martineau would be staying at the château

until the day of the wedding. Mrs. Koster explained that many of the other guests, distant cousins and old friends, most of whom were older people, would be arriving every day and would also be staying at the château until after the wedding. Each guest, of course, would be bringing gifts, along with best wishes for the happiness of the bride and groom in the future.

Marion was listening with only one ear. The greater part of her mind was preoccupied with the dream she had had so often. All the guests gathered for the wedding, laughing and talking, and then the faces suddenly changing from joy to sorrow and consternation. The rumor being whispered around the room, "There is no wedding. There will be no wedding!"

"What's on your mind?" asked Isabel sharply. "You seem to be a long way off."

"She's probably dreaming . . . which is easy enough to understand," Mrs. Koster said kindly.

"I'm sorry," Marion murmured, trying to control a shudder.

"No need to apologize, my dear. But I would suggest that you make yourself especially beautiful for lunch. Perhaps you might even wear one of the new dresses you've just brought back from Paris. Julia is always very interested in the lastest fashions."

Isabel snorted in spite, as she always did every time Mrs. Martineau's name was mentioned. It was quite evident she had a particular dislike for the woman.

"Of course." Marion smiled affectionately. "I'll be happy to do it, if you want me to."

"Oh, surely not just for me. I would think the important thing is to please your fiancé."

Marion smiled, hoping it was the smile of a bride-to-be, five days before her wedding.

"Let's hope it will be a nice day Saturday," Isabel said. "The bride on which the sun shines is assured of a life of happiness."

"Don't be silly," Mrs. Koster said, her tone a mixture of annoyance and indulgence. "Those old sayings have no meaning. Of course, Isabel, I know you're just as concerned as any one of us about the future happiness of these two."

There was a spark of joy in her sad eyes when Isabel answered proudly, "Jeremy's well-being means more to me than anything in the world, Martha."

Finally the meal was over. It seemed as if everyone without saying so, wanted only to get back to his or her own room. In the hall outside Marion's room Jeremy took her in his arms. Again she managed to avoid his kiss, and she was relieved that he didn't insist.

"Good night, my darling," he said simply. "Sweet dreams."

Marion undressed and climbed wearily between her silk sheets. She hoped she would fall asleep as quickly as possible. Tiger had already found his way into her room and was sleeping on the foot of the bed. Comforted by his presence and overwhelmed with exhaustion, she was soon in a deep sleep.

Suddenly she was wide awake. There were footsteps outside the door to her room. She sat up in bed and looked at the luminous dial of her clock on the bedside table. It was 12:30 A.M. She had been in bed for about two hours. At this hour usually everyone at Grunberg was in bed, asleep. Who could be walking around the house at this time of night?

Jeremy's room was at the far end of the hallway, separated from hers by several rooms and the library. There was a stairway at that end of the hall that Jeremy normally used. There was no need for him to take the stairway at Marion's end of the hallway. Jeremy, Isabel and Marion were the only ones with rooms on this floor of the château. In order to avoid unnecessary exertion, Mrs. Koster had taken a suite of rooms on the main floor. Marion jumped out of bed and padded over to the door in her bare feet and silently opened it. The hallway was dark and deserted. There was no light, nor was there anyone in sight. Yet Marion could have sworn that she had just heard someone walking in

front of her door, causing the floorboards to creak.
someone must be hiding. Who? She stayed there for a
few moments, looking and listening, but she heard and
saw nothing. No light came from the direction of Jeremy's room, and Isabel's room seemed dark and silent,
too. Tiger leaped from the bed and began to rub against
her legs. Marion picked up the cat and went back to bed.
In no time they were both fast asleep once more.

Outside a storm was raging, the wind attacking the
walls of the château with incredible force. Every so
often a bolt of lightning pierced the sky followed by the
deep rumble of thunder.

WHEN MARION WOKE UP the next morning the storm was
over, but the sky was overcast and it was still raining.
After sharing her breakfast with Tiger, which had
become something of a ritual, she got dressed and
prepared to go downstairs.

She wondered how she would spend the morning. In
this weather she couldn't go out for a walk and she
didn't feel like reading. For that matter she didn't feel
like doing much of anything. She stayed in her room
for a while, looking out the window. Tiger, trying to
say, "Thank you for breakfast," in the only way he
knew how, was rubbing himself against her legs, purring loudly. It suddenly occured to her that this would
be a perfect morning to pay a visit to Marguerite and
Beth.

Preceded by the cat, who seemed immediately to
understand her intention, she retraced the route she
had taken before. Once again she found the two old
women sitting close to the stove, sipping coffee gener-
ously laced with cognac. Neither seemed at all surprised to see Marion.

"Ah, here's Marion," said Marguerite simply.

She got up and offered Marion the same Louis XV
blue-velvet chair, which seemed to be reserved for
visitors. "Here, sit down."

It was somewhat cold and damp in the other rooms of

the château, but here the room was warm and pleasant, enhanced by the aroma of coffee and the spices and herbs that were suspended from the ceiling. Following the protocol of simple hospitality, Marguerite immediately invited Marion to join them in a cup of coffee.

"Thank you, I will," replied Marion.

As she sipped the delicious brew, the two old women sat quietly looking at her. Were they able to see more than what appeared on the surface? Could they sense her inner turmoil? As though someone had signaled her to go ahead, Marion began to speak. "I'm sure you must feel as dreadful as I do about Ida's death," she said.

"What a sad girl," exclaimed Marguerite. "Well, she certainly has paid very dearly for her mistakes."

Somewhat surprised by the answer Marion continued, "I also heard about Leon Altamira being arrested."

"He was released," said Beth. News of events in the village and surrounding area reached them almost daily by the way of the various merchants and delivery boys who came to the château. "If the manager had been guilty, the mayor, who is one of Ida's relatives, certainly would never have allowed him to be set free," Beth continued. "Anyway, Leon had no reason to be jealous. He could have had Ida back anytime. All he had to do was lift a finger and she would have jumped at the chance to go back to him. He wasn't the one to whom Ida was an embarrassment."

"Be quiet, Beth," Marguerite said.

It might have been that Beth had put a little too much cognac in her coffee. At any rate she was very talkative and none too discreet about what she was saying. Beth blinked her eyes, stared at Marguerite for a moment, then shrugged her shoulders.

"I have a right to my own opinion," she said petulantly. "I know a lot of things."

"Do you really? And just what are these things you think you know? You should mind your own business and let the law take care of it."

Smoke escaped from the fire roaring in the stove and climbed the walls. From time to time there was a loud crack and a fiery ember leaped against the protective grill.

"Please," Marion interjected, "don't quarrel."

"Marguerite," Beth continued, oblivious to Marion's plea, "I think we should tell—"

"No!" Marguerite exclaimed with a vehemence that startled Marion.

Marguerite shook her head. There was an atmosphere of mystery in the smoky room. Crouched on a chair, the cat blinked his golden eyes...and listened. Marion put a hand to her forehead. The smoky atmosphere, made even more heavy by the various aromas and the brandy in her coffee, was beginning to get to her. *What is Marguerite hiding*, Marion wondered. *Why won't she let Beth talk? And what does Beth know?* Marion was about to press for information—something told her that whatever it was, it was important—when Marguerite changed the subject.

"Besides, Beth, dear," she said in a soothing voice accompanied by an admonishing frown, "I'm sure Marion has come to talk to us about her wedding dress."

Marion smiled. "Yes, I have. Could I bring it to you this afternoon?"

"Of course," Marguerite smiled, and Marion was pleased to see that Beth was smiling and nodding, too. Arrangements made, Marion left the room, taking with her the impression that something had been said that concerned her, something important...but she didn't know exactly what it was.

There was still time before the guests would be arriving for lunch. Marion decided to go to her room and get ready.

To keep her mind busy she opened the closet to choose what she would wear to lunch. After a good deal of consideration, she decided on a dress of classic design, made of fine, silver-gray silk highlighted with splashes of shocking pink. With its simple straight line, and long narrow sleeves, the dress had an Oriental look about it. The neckline was cut low. She decided she would wear her hair swept up, baring a neck as slim and fragile as the stem of a wild flower.

Slipping the dress over her head, Marion stood in front of the mirror and examined herself very seriously, as if she were looking at a stranger. The image in the mirror seemed familiar and yet, at the same time, somewhat strange. It was as if another woman, quite new to her, had taken up residence inside her—a woman who was considerably more beautiful.

After looking at herself for a few minutes Marion decided that the neckline of her dress was a little too low, considering that one of the guests at lunch was to be a priest. She took a gossamer silk scarf from her drawer, and draped it around her neck.

She noticed that the rain had stopped. From her window she could see the sun shining on the treetops, the emerald green grass and the colorful flower beds. She opened the window and heard the birds singing; their songs were joyful. She took a deep breath, inhaling the sweet air.

The scents of the forest reaching me are the same as those reaching Leon, she thought. *He's only a few steps away. The path to his cottage starts right there, in that small dark area. I can see it from here. If I were to go there, the dog would bark. If I knocked on his door, it would open and I would see him standing in the doorway. I would see those dark eyes. What would he say?*

She was talking to herself like a person in a dream. Softly she repeated his name. *Leon.* Each small insect that buzzed by, each leaf trembling in the breeze, each bird winging in air seemed to be whispering his name. "If I went to see him...talked to him," she murmured.

She was aching inside. She raised her hands to her burning cheeks. "I must be losing my mind," she said aloud. "What am I thinking of? What's happening to me?"

Suddenly she knew she had to see Leon, to talk to him. She had to know the truth...and he was the only one who could tell her.

Chapter 13

Marion threw a cashmere shawl over her shoulders and in a few seconds, she was downstairs. In the hallway she met Jeanne. The young maid stared at her in surprise. As she stepped aside to let Marion pass, she asked, "Are you going out?"

Marion hardly stopped to reply. "Yes. I have a headache. I'm just going for a walk to get some fresh air."

"Don't forget that guests are expected for lunch soon."

The words seemed almost like an accusation to Marion, who was trembling with eagerness to get away. Would there be time to see Leon and still be back for lunch? She didn't care.

As the puzzled maid watched her walk away, wondering, perhaps even criticizing the strange behavior of this woman from Paris, Marion hurried across the lawn to the path that led to Leon's house.

For the moment her mind was occupied with only one thing—nothing else mattered. In a few minutes she was at the house, the dog barking as she approached. There was no other sound. She hesitated for a moment, afraid that the house might be empty. Quickly she walked across the clearing and knocked on the door. She waited, her heart pounding in her ears.

A few moments went by. Was Leon inside? Was he deciding whether or not to show himself? There was the sound of a chair scraping the floor as it was moved back and footsteps could be heard approaching the door. The door opened and Leon appeared, wearing khaki trousers and a short-sleeved sport shirt, holding his dog by the collar.

"Marion!" He stared at the graceful figure in the elegant silk dress, the pale, oval face, the gray eyes and long lashes, the fine forehead emphasized by her up-swept hair. He looked as if he couldn't believe his eyes. "What a surprise," he said finally. "A visit from you was the farthest thing from my mind." He couldn't understand it at all. Seeing his confusion, Marion wondered if her visit was a cause for joy or, perhaps, annoyance.

There was an awkward pause. Having been freed, the dog cautiously approached Marion. Apparently satisfied that the visitor was more friend than enemy, Satan returned to his favorite spot at his master's feet.

Stepping politely to one side, Leon invited Marion in. The door opened on a single large room, entirely masculine in decor. The walls had been whitewashed and several guns hung alongside different kinds of hunting gear. On a sideboard of sculptured wood, an antique clock ticked away the minutes. In front of the window was a large desk laden with a typewriter, books, piles of documents and other papers. *Is that where he works on his articles and books—the research papers Martha Koster had mentioned*, Marion wondered.

Everything in the room seemed functional, suggesting that Leon was accustomed to leading a life of hard work, study and productivity. There was also, however, an air of some refinement. All of the furnishings in the room were antiques, obviously authentic and quite beautiful. There were numerous shelves filled with books, and the two great chairs, one on either side of the fireplace, were upholstered in the finest leather.

"Please sit down," said Leon in a quiet voice, indicating a chair. He himself did not sit.

He was as tall and virile as Marion remembered him, and yet there was something quite different about his expression today.

"And to what do I owe this unexpected pleasure?"

He seemed to be in full possession of himself. He was quite polite, but at the same time distant. And he knew very well how to hide surprise, embarrassment, perhaps even irritation.

"I—I came..." stammered Marion. "I came...."

Now she couldn't find the words to explain the reasons that had brought her here. Then she rushed to voice her thoughts before her courage failed her completely.

"I've come to tell you that I know all about your recent...problems. I am concerned. I couldn't believe what I heard. No...I couldn't believe that you would be capable of any part of this horrible crime."

Altamira stood leaning on the mantelpiece, appearing to be listening intently. He nodded his head.

"Thank you," he said. "I'm touched to know of your concern. It's very kind of you to take the time to come and tell me, especially now, when you must be very busy with the preparations for your wedding." He paused briefly before going on. "You're getting married this coming Saturday, aren't you?"

Somewhat taken aback, she murmured yes.

They were both silent for a moment. A strange kind of tension seemed to fill the atmosphere. Then, in the same quiet tone, he continued, "I really am touched. You are preoccupied with love and your coming marriage. You must be blessed with a very special kind of generosity to be able to forget your world for long enough to bring comfort to another man. Your expression of confidence is something I'm not likely ever to forget."

Marion clasped her hands together; her engagement ring and the beautiful emerald ring were quite visible. "'Preoccupied with love...'" she repeated musingly. "That's a strange kind of thing to say. Why do you put it that way?"

"Well, you love Jeremy, don't you? You've told me often enough. Have you changed your mind, perhaps?" He was leaning forward, his face close to hers. Suddenly he straightened up and with an abrupt movement, took a pipe from the rack hanging on the wall. His movements slow and deliberate now, he began to fill it with tobacco. But instead of lighting the pipe, he took a few steps toward the young woman and spoke with concern in his voice.

"Are you as uncertain about your feelings as you seem to be? I need—" And then he stopped. Shaking his head, he turned, walked to the other chair and sat down. "Forgive me," he sighed. "Although it may be weak for me to say I am exhausted, I have to say it."

Marion then realized how desperately tired Leon looked. The expression on his face was a mixture of pain and bitterness. His eyes seemed quite sunken and it was obvious that he was very tense. Marion longed to tell him that it worried her to see him this way—but she said nothing.

Thinking she knew the reason for these changes in him she murmured, "You were in love with Ida, weren't you?"

He looked at her for a moment, then turned away.

"Yes," he said in a low voice. "There was a time when I loved Ida. At least, I thought I loved her. You know, sometimes it is no more than whimsy, an adventure...even an illusion. Unfortunately it's often very hard to tell one from the other."

The pendulum of the clock swung back and forth relentlessly. The dog twitched slightly and whined in his sleep from the braided rug in front of the fireplace. After a pause Leon continued in the same quiet voice.

"Men say that the ideal woman," he said slowly, "simply doesn't exist. We say this, of course, because most of us never find her. Or, if we do, it is only to find that she is unavailable...inaccessible. and yet, finding her is the stuff of which dreams are made. So, knowing that she does exist, we dream...even though such dreaming may lead to nothing more than pain and suffering. Just to have known her sometimes must be enough...and never something to be regretted."

He was speaking in an absentminded way, yet with a certain degree of intensity. His eyes, when they met hers, gave her a shock of painful intimacy that forced Marion to look away. What was he trying to say? She could see the flame burning deep in his dark eyes and she would have given everything to know the reason for his sorrow.

"Yes," Leon went on. "I thought I loved Ida. She was beautiful and spirited. But I was not experienced enough in the ways of love to recognize what was true feeling and what was not. In reality it was no more than an affair. I was caught up in the kind of infatuation that women like Ida seem to inspire so easily. And yet, I would have married her. Men, you see, can be such fools...and I would not have been the first man to have made that kind of mistake."

He got up from his chair and began to pace around the room, his step uncertain. Turning to face Marion, he continued. "But I was not the only man to notice Ida...to find her beautiful. Actually, it's an old story...and very ordinary." He smiled bitterly. "I began to see through the fog of infatuation. I suspect Ida guessed that my feelings were changing. It is hard to know for sure. In any case she quickly found another 'friend.' The other man had more charm, more prestige, and certainly more money than I. At that point it was child's play for him to take Ida away from me. My relationship with her was an honest one and I would have given her my name. Such was never the intention of the other man. Foolishly, Ida thought she could bring him around to marrying her and was very disappointed when she learned that he had other plans. He told her quite bluntly that their relationship was over and didn't concern himself with the obvious consequences of their short-lived romance. The poor girl pleaded with him, but it was useless. Before long he even refused to speak to her. It was then that Ida came to me for help. She wanted to keep the child, but she needed protection and support; it was then that she asked me to marry her."

Understanding quite clearly what he was trying to say Marion murmured, "Is that why she was here the day I came?"

He nodded his head and sighed. "Ida was very sure of her beauty," he said, "but she wasn't very bright."

He paced a few more steps, stopped, came back to look at Marion. "She had never known me to be anything but kind. And certainly, with Ida, I was always indulgent. So she thought that all she had to do was come back and I would be overcome by her charm and help her cover up her mistake. But I'm not a saint. She was asking too much. When she finally realized that she wasn't going to be able to convince me, she left in despair. I never saw her again. She must have thrown herself into the Green Pond, preferring, as the saying goes, death to dishonor."

He stopped for a moment and appeared lost in thought. "I am," he resumed thoughtfully, "responsible to a degree, I think, for her pregnancy and for her death. I can't help but think that had my feelings been more sure, more real, she wouldn't have gotten involved in such a dead-end relationship, wouldn't have been so desperate to marry. And," he concluded, a note of anguish creeping into his voice, "if I hadn't turned her away the way I did, she might be alive today."

Marion looked at his face, saw the self-contempt in those dark eyes and could not remain silent. "But Ida did not commit suicide, as you seem to think," she exclaimed.

He looked at her in amazement. "But that's the only thing I can possibly believe."

"Nor could you marry a woman you didn't love," she continued firmly.

She could feel the anger in her rising. It was quite clear that he was suffering because of Ida's death and she couldn't bear to see him suffer.

"Had I married Ida," he said, "it would have been an

act of charity. Unfortunately I couldn't find it in myself to be quite charitable enough. Nevertheless there must have been some other way I could have helped her. I would have found it, had other considerations, other feelings not come into it to interfere with my judgment. If I had brought the practical help to Ida that she needed, I would have been risking something else...would have risked destroying it. I was caught in a dilemma. Such decisions can be very difficult. I wish I could be sure that I acted in the best possible way."

Now it was Leon who was searching for the right words.

"I asked you on several occasions, including just a little while ago," he resumed hesitantly, "if you really loved Jeremy. If you do love him and if he loves you, you will be as happy as you deserve to be. That is my only reason for asking you so often. I want to know that you will be happy."

The conversation suddenly seemed to be heading in a very different direction and his words seemed to follow no logical course. And yet what he was saying touched the very heart of the problem that was tormenting both of them.

They looked at each other. This time there was no anger, no hostility. In Leon's eyes shone a very soft, somehow sad light. "How innocent and pure you look," he said suddenly. "I pray that nothing ugly or evil will ever touch you."

His voice was warm and gentle, and yet resonant.

He leaned toward the young woman and she could feel his breath against her cheek. It was as though she had been touched by fire. She felt she was choking and in a gesture that seemed quite unconscious she removed the silk scarf from around her neck.

Leon's eyes, which had been filled with joy and admiration only a moment before, now stared at a very definite point near her shoulder. "What's that mark on your shoulder? A scar?" he asked.

Slightly annoyed by his sudden preoccupation with

something that seemed to be totally irrelevant to the emotion of the moment Marion replied, "A birthmark. Just a birthmark."

Leon lifted his hand to his own collar, in what appeared to be an attempt to close it tight around his neck and continued to stare at the small cloverleaf completely fascinated by it.

"I must go," Marion said, feeling acutely uneasy. "It's getting late and they're expecting me for lunch."

The manager blinked his eyes, as though he had just awakened from a deep sleep. "Yes," he said, "you should go."

He took a handkerchief from his pocket and wiped his face.

"Forgive me," he said. "I must be alone. I need time to think. As I said before, I'm completely exhausted...."

"I understand," murmured Marion.

In truth she didn't understand at all. Why had she come here? Suddenly she was overcome by a feeling of profound disappointment.

"I won't bother you anymore," she said.

She headed for the door, then stopped and turned to look one last time at the room around her. She wanted to fix in her mind forever the picture of this room, the dog, the man whose face seemed to express such profound concern. He made no move, no sign, no gesture to stop her as she opened the door and walked out.

Chapter 14

In a daze, Marion ran all the way back to the château. Her mind was filled with unanswered questions, and out of the confusion, few words came back to her. She tried in vain to make some sense of it all. She couldn't. She simply couldn't understand what Leon had been saying and she was left with a feeling of uncertainty.

Back at the château Marion ran into Isabel, who appeared to have been watching out for her. She grabbed Marion by the arm. "Where were you?" she asked roughly. "Apparently you've forgotten about time. Mrs. Martineau is here. The priest won't be coming. He sent a message to say that he had to make an emergency sick call. Oh, well, we can get along without him—as long as he's available to perform the ceremony on Saturday."

She spoke with such authority, Marion was taken completely by surprise. Behind the mask of a silly old fool there existed quite another kind of woman, a woman who was very sure of herself and filled with determination.

But there was no time to protest. The next thing Marion knew, she was being steered into the living room where Mrs. Koster and Mrs. Martineau were waiting.

"Well! Here's the happy bride-to-be!" cried Mrs. Martineau. She jumped up from her chair and embraced Marion with vigor. Since Marion had last seen her in her elegant store, she had changed the color of her hair; now, it was ash blond. Her makeup was still liberally applied.

"How pretty you are, my dear," she said ecstatically. "And that dress, it's incredible. the scarf adds *just* the right touch. Chic, my dear...too, too chic."

Mrs. Martineau's dress was a shade of pink. In itself the dress was quite lovely, but it would have been much more appropriate on an eighteen-year-old. With undiminished enthusiasm she went on, "My dear, I just love your scarf! But it would be much more flattering draped just so...."

Without warning she reached out and rearranged the scarf around Marion's neck, revealing the small brown birthmark.

Suddenly quite nervous, Isabel frowned and rubbed her hands together. She jumped up from her chair and busily pulled and poked at Marion to arrange the scarf to her own liking. Although somewhat taken aback by Isabel's unexpected interference, Mrs. Martineau kept on talking, apparently resuming the conversation she and Mrs. Koster had been having previously. "Marion, Martha was saying that there's to be no marriage contract."

Marion nodded. "Jeremy doesn't see any need for one."

The visitor, very much aware of all the ins and outs of marriage from her own previous experience, observed, "When there's no marriage contract, the law of community property prevails. This will mean that you will own half of what is his, automatically and, of course, vice versa. I must say I find this very generous on Jeremy's part...certainly, proof enough of his love. Who says chivalry is dead, that love no longer exists in this world?"

"Oh, love has always existed, Julia," observed Mrs.

Koster softly. "It always will. And where love exists, money becomes unimportant. I agree with Jeremy wholeheartedly. There is no fortune in this world that could ever compare to the value of a woman such as Marion."

Marion blushed. The subject of this conversation had more obvious significance for these experienced women of the world than it had for her. Jeremy had mentioned the matter only briefly to her and she was vague about the meaning of it all. What did it all matter, anyway. She and Jeremy would marry and share their lives together—forever.

"Well, knowing how conservative Jeremy usually is, Martha, it's nice to see him being so sentimental for a change," Mrs. Martineau sighed with satisfaction.

Taking Marion's hand, Mrs. Martineau made the expected complimentary remarks about her engagement ring. Then, she gasped and looked at her friend. "Why, Martha!" she exclaimed, "I see you've given Marion the Sayn emerald. The talisman." She turned to Marion. "It will bring you happiness, my child. You're going to be very happy."

"Yes," murmured Marion. "I will be happy."

She wondered, as she said these words, why she should be feeling so sad, but Julia left little opportunity for introspection. She now was asking about the section of the château that was being renovated to make an apartment for the young couple and was expected to be ready by the time Marion and Jeremy got home from their honeymoon in Italy.

"I hope you'll show me through it tomorrow," said Mrs. Martineau.

"You'll have to ask Jeremy, " replied Marion. "I'd be glad to show it to you, but he's insisting on surprising me."

Marion blushed. Since she had first arrived at Grunberg, she had wanted to choose the colors for paint, wallpaper and drapes and select the furniture from the beautiful pieces Mrs. Koster had offered to place at her disposal. After all, she would be spending the rest of her life with these things. But Jeremy remained firm, and recently she had stopped bothering about it. Somehow she had become quite indifferent to her own future.

At that moment the person whose unselfishness and generosity had been the subject of such admiration came into the room. Jeremy greeted Mrs. Martineau gallantly, bowed before his stepmother and kissed her hand, and then moved quickly to kiss Marion on the cheek and hold her hand in both of his.

"Your fiancée is lovely," said Mrs. Martineau. "You're a fortunate man, Jeremy."

Jeremy smiled and squeezed Marion's hand, gracefully settling onto the sofa beside her.

"Happiness appears to become her," continued the visitor gaily. "I've never seen such lovely eyes. She's going to be a beautiful bride."

Jeremy turned to look at Marion. "Did you have a good day, darling?"

She simply nodded her head in reply. Not to speak is not to lie. In any case, what else could she have answered?

Mrs. Martineau adjusted her skirt and then observed, "You're just as handsome as ever, dear boy, but you do look a little haggard. You're going to have to do something about that. A bridegroom must be at his very best, you know."

"Indeed!" said Jeremy, forcing a smile. "I'll look after it, don't worry. I'm on vacation starting tomorrow. I won't be going back to the factory until we're home from our honeymoon. They'll just have to manage without me."

Abruptly, he changed the subject. "Isn't the priest here yet?"

This time it was Isabel who spoke up. "He won't be coming. He's making a sick call instead, apparently."

Something in Isabel's tone of voice prompted Martha to say, "Well, I think he's to be admired for resisting the temptation of a good dinner to attend to his duty. I don't feel offended at all that he hasn't come."

Isabel bit her lip and looked at Jeremy. Scowling, he returned the look. Were they able to read each other's thoughts? It was not the first time Marion had noticed what seemed to be some secret form of communication between her fiancé and his cousin, and it troubled her.

Jeanne entered to announce that luncheon was ready, and they all made their way to the dining room.

Sitting beside him, Marion looked at Jeremy, his handsome profile and blond head outlined against the background of an old tapestry depicting hunters and horses, birds and leaves in varying shades of blue. She admired his elegance, his good looks, but she felt no urge to be close to him, no warmth at the thought that soon he would be her husband. Nothing about him touched her heart.

Suddenly her confusion and distress became tragically clear. She was able to understand the reason for her torment, the feeling of uneasiness that had been troubling her. Quite simply, she didn't love Jeremy anymore. Had she ever really loved him? Had she mistaken the need to be loved for love itself? Had she been fascinated by this handsome, wealthy man whose greatest attraction, perhaps had been that he had made her the envy of all her co-workers?

Little by little, the enchantment had faded. The wonder of those marvelous first days had gradually disappeared like the burst of light of fireworks blazing for a few moments against the dark of a night sky. Stunned, Marion felt weak with the terrible truth that had suddenly dawned on her. When? How had it happened? How could she have made such a terrible mistake? Might things have been different, might she have loved him if he had not been so cold, so very much in control of himself? His inability to show true affection and warmth had discouraged her. And yet...she had to love him. She *had* to love him, because he loved her and he wanted to marry her—even though she was without a name, without money, without position.

But the magic was gone. No matter what she tried to tell herself, the fact remained that she no longer loved him. Now it was quite a different man she loved. A man whose face was tanned, whose hair was dark red, whose elegance was the grace of a wild animal of the forest and whose dark, flashing eyes knew how to glow with the soft warmth of affection. Now she knew why her heart felt the way it did and she faced it openly. But having faced it, she was still left with the question of what to do about it. She felt like a fly caught in a spider's web. Should she tell Jeremy the truth and cancel the wedding? She could imagine the scandal that would be caused of she were to break the engagement, especially since it was only three days before the wedding. People would talk and rumors would be flying around the village. The newspapers, too, would have a heyday.

No. She couldn't put Jeremy through that. It would humiliate him, which would be quite unforgivable. The disgrace would be too great, impossible to explain. Neither could she show such ingratitude to Mrs. Koster, who had been so generous and good to her, who had treated her almost like a daughter even before she had become part of the family. It could even hurt her health, which was already so fragile. The shock, perhaps, could even kill her, a possibility that Marion could not bear. She would regret it for the rest of her life.

No, Marion told herself. *I can't do it.*

She had a strong sense of honor and great respect for a given promise. Even more important were the kindnesses she had accepted, the gifts and the affection she had received and returned.

Although she had now come to realize that she did not love Jeremy, she still felt grateful to him for choosing her to be his wife. She had no choice—she had to go through with the wedding. But when she walked up the aisle to the altar, she would not be the happy bride the wedding guests had come to see.

Throughout the luncheon Marion managed to keep herself under control. Mrs. Martineau, meanwhile, talked nonstop, leaving little opportunity for anyone else to say much of anything.

"Well," she exclaimed at one point during lunch, "when are you going to fill me in on what's been happening? The people in the village are going wild gossiping. Last rumor had it that Ida Somers was murdered by the mayor's wife, which just goes to show how wrong rumors can be. But the newspapers don't say much, even though they manage to fill page after page with the story every day."

"Oh," said Mrs. Koster with a sigh, "it is such an unfortunate incident. But we don't know any more than anyone else."

"I understand the police at first thought she had drowned, but it seems she'd been strangled."

"Yes."

With the curiosity of a person who finds stimulation in the most morbid items to be found in newspapers, Mrs. Martineau asked Jeremy, "Did you know her?"

"Yes," replied Jeremy, his voice strangely flat. "She worked at the factory." He put down the glass he had been holding in his hand. "I had just fired her," he went on in the same odd tone. "We weren't satisfied with her work."

Stubborn in her incomprehensible dislike for the unfortunate Ida, Isabel grumbled, "She was of absolutely no consequence. She doesn't deserve to be pitied."

"Poor girl," murmured Mrs. Koster.

"Some say that a lover was involved," persisted Mrs. Martineau.

Anticipating the mention of Leon, Marion began to tremble.

"People always talk," replied Mrs. Koster, "but usually that's all it is—talk."

The breeze wafting through the open windows moved the curtains. It was almost as if the restless shadow of the young woman in the red dress had slipped into the room and was moving noiselessly from place to place seeking shelter. Marion thought about her strange conversation with Marguerite and Beth early that morning. What were they hiding? What did they know that Marguerite was refusing to tell? Marion resolved to try to find out when she went to show them her dress after lunch.

When the meal was over, it was time to admire the gift Mrs. Martineau had brought, a magnificent ewer finely sculpted of solid silver.

"It's beautiful," said Jeremy. "A collector's piece."

Mrs. Martineau beamed with pride. "It's very old. From the sixteenth century, in fact."

"You spoil us, Julia."

"It's lovely," murmured Marion. "Thank you very much, Mrs. Martineau."

"You're very welcome, my dear," replied Mrs. Martineau. "It's such a pleasure to be witness to a true love marriage." Dreamily she added, "Really...love is the only thing in life."

Jeremy did not say a word. He seemed worried and preoccupied. *Is he aware of what is going on in my mind,* Marion wondered. Filled with sudden remorse, Marion caught Jeremy's eye and smiled at him, hoping that she would be able to make him feel better. Would she be doing this for the rest of her life? Smiling to cover up her real feelings? Smiling because she felt guilty?

After a polite period of socializing following the elegant lunch, Martha confessed to needing to lie down.

"But please, Julia, you young ones, Isabel, please carry on."

"Well, Martha," Julia responded cheerfully, "I wouldn't mind a rest myself."

"Fine, dear. I'll have Jeanne show you to your suite. And to all of you, good afternoon."

Marion was relieved. She had found it very difficult to maintain a happy face in spite of what she was feeling inside. She needed to get away, to think, to rest, to be herself. And in a short time, she would have to go see Marguerite and Beth.

She excused herself and climbed the wide, polished oak stairs to the second floor. Wearily she pushed open the door to her room. Its elegant interior didn't comfort her this time. Overcome by sobs, she sank into an overstuffed armchair and buried her face in her hends.

She tried to keep from thinking about Leon, but it was no use. Leon didn't love her. And even if he did it wouldn't change anything. Marion searched for a solution to her problem, knowing that there was no solution. Her thoughts kept spinning back to her visit with Leon that morning. With a surge of feeling she remembered the comforting atmosphere of his home, the warmth and tenderness in his dark eyes. Again she tried to piece the puzzle together. What had he meant? What was he trying to say? Why was it so important?

Inside her heart was crying out, "Save me...save me." Despair and resignation were struggling in her soul. Through the window of her room she could see the sun hanging in the midday sky, but dark clouds were lining the horizon like a funeral procession. It was a languid afternoon, and the sound of birds singing mingled with the mournful howl of a dog in the distance. *Is it Satan,* Marion wondered tearfully.

With a start she remembered the time and rose from her chair. Automatically moving, like a woman who preferred not to think about the significance of her actions, she went to the closet and carefully took down her wedding dress. She looked around the room for something to cover it with. In spite of everything she wasn't going to forget the small details of life—she didn't want Jeremy to see the dress before the ceremony. But she could find nothing suitable. Even the boxes had been taken away. She decided to slip down the stairs as quickly as she could, hoping that no one would see her.

Quietly she opened the door, the voluminous featherlight silk rustling with her movement. There was no one in the hall or on the stairs, but at the foot of the stairs, just as she was about to cross the hall to the door that would lead her to Marguerite's rooms, she was startled by a dark shadow in the doorway.

"Marion, darling, why do you jump?"

It was Jeremy, the one person Marion did not want to see.

"Don't look, Jeremy," Marion cautioned. "I'm going to see Marguerite and Beth about something for my dress."

"Well—I've seen it now," Jeremy said, blocking Marion's way. "Here, let me have a closer look."

Gossamer folds floated in the air as he held the dress out in front of him. His eyes darkened with anger. "I thought I told you to be sure to have a closed neck. But look at this! How could you, Marion?"

"But Jeremy—"

"You deliberately went against my wishes," he said cuttingly.

"Jeremy, what's wrong?" Marion cried her nerves stretched to breaking point. "Why are you being so unreasonable?"

Jeremy stared at her in silence. "Very well, then," he finally said. "I didn't know I was being 'so unreasonable' as you put it. I asked only one thing. I insisted on a modest neckline. I don't think that's too much for a bridegroom to ask. Perhaps Marguerite can help you."

"Jeremy, it will ruin the dress—"

"What does that matter? My feelings are more important. And this is *very* important. That's all I have to say about it, Marion. Goodbye." Turning abruptly, he strode down the hallway and through the door.

Marion stood immobile, her beautiful dress draped over her arm. She no longer felt like crying.

THE WARM AND CHEERFUL ATMOSPHERE in Marguerite's room didn't revive Marion. She did her best to seem her normal self, but she could tell from the looks in Marguerite's and Beth's eyes that they knew something was seriously bothering her. After both women had admired the dress profusely over several cups of coffee,

Marguerite spoke. "Marion," she began gently, obviously feeling a bit hesitant. "You're not happy about something. Please—can you talk to us about it? We might be able to help. And at least it may make you feel better."

Marion looked into Marguerite's honest blue eyes. She so yearned to talk to someone, but....

"Oh, Marguerite," Beth interjected in a teasing tone, "I bet she's afraid that we would spill the beans—aren't you, dear?"

"Oh, no," Marion said with a weak smile. "There's nothing wrong. It's just all the excitement."

"Now, Marion. Don't think Beth and I have been around all these years without learning a thing or two about people," Marguerite said, getting up to put a frail old arm around Marion's shoulder. Tiger, snuggled happily in Marion's lap, began to purr loudly.

"Oh," Marion sighed. The warmth of this room, of Tiger and these two, very dear old women was too much for her. She could hold back her tears no longer. Like a dam bursting, she broke into sobs. The two women hovered around her, bringing handkerchiefs for her tears, a cup of tea and gentle, reassuring pats to comfort her.

Marion looked through her tears at their affectionate, expectant faces. "I—I'm so sorry. It's just that .... It's.... I—I—I don't love Jeremy," she finally burst out, tears choking her. "I don't know what to do," she cried, her words like a desperate plea.

There was an uncanny silence in the room. Even Tiger was no longer purring. Marguerite looked at Beth and then back at Marion.

"Are you sure, Marion? Sometimes people get scared just before they get married. They start thinking that it is a big mistake and all sorts of things—but that passes."

Marion shook her head. "I used to think it was like that. But I was wrong. It's not. I had only known Jeremy for one week when he proposed to me. It all happened so fast. And it was so romantic. No other man had ever loved me. I guess I was sort of swept off my feet by it all. But then he changed. Or I guess I should say that I think I started to know him better....I don't love him, that's all."

Marion paused, her tears rolling down her cheeks. "What can I do? Nothing! I—I feel like dying."

She buried her head in her lap, and trembled with the weight of her unhappiness. Then she looked up and wiped her face. "Anyway, why should I be bothering you with this? I will marry Jeremy and I will learn to love him. Many women have had much worse lives. Why should I expect so much?"

Marguerite turned and looked at Beth. Finally they nodded at each other. Marguerite stood up, walked to a dresser and opened a small drawer in the upper right corner. Marion watched her with curiosity. For a second the woman hesitated, and then, with obvious determination, she reached into the far corner of the drawer and drew out a small leather-covered box of the size that would hold a necklace. Slowly, and with a look of pained apprehension on her face, she came back to her chair and eased herself into its soft down-filled depths.

Marion had become so preoccupied by the old woman's mysterious movements that she had forgotten her tears. "What are you doing, Marguerite?" she asked with a nervous laugh.

Marguerite looked at her soberly. "Marion, I wish we didn't have to show you this...but Beth and I feel that we must now."

Marion fell silent. Suddenly she was frightened. Something in Marguerite's manner warned her that she should brace herself, that the pain she was feeling now might be nothing, compared to....

Marguerite pulled a key out from around her neck and handed it along with the box to Beth. "Here, Beth," she said with a cold expression. "You do the honors."

With haste, as if to get the distasteful matter over

with as quickly as possible, Beth opened the box and handed the small piece of paper inside to Marion.

Wordlessly, Marion quickly unfolded it. It was a sheet of paper that had been torn from a small notepad. It was covered with loose, childlike writing. Without thinking, Marion began to read. The words jumped at her.

Dear Jeremy, you don't want to see me anymore. You don't return my calls. I'm forbidden to go into the factory. I've written you letters, but you haven't answered. Perhaps you didn't get them. To make sure this note reaches you, I'm going to take it to the château myself and give it to someone to hand to you personally.

Jeremy, you can't marry this girl from Paris. I am the one you must marry. It is your *duty*. I'm not good at expressing myself, being just a simple girl, but you're a gentleman and you found me very much to your taste at one time. Now you have no right to abandon me.

I must see you. It's urgent! I'll wait for you tonight on the path that leads to the Green Pond. Please, you must come.

                                        Yours very unhappily, Ida.

P.S. If you don't come, I'll talk to your fiancée. Believe me, I'll tell her everything. If necessary I'll even wait at the church and confront both of you with the truth.

Sitting on the floor in a patch of sunlight, Tiger was carefully smoothing his ruffled coat. From time to time he would stop, a paw in midair, and look at Marion. A mild breeze coming through the open window caused the piece of paper on Marion's knee to flutter. She sat unmoving, eyes staring blankly, as though hypnotized by the words she had just read. Her head was in a turmoil. Gradually the horrible meaning of the written words was starting to reach her. Events and circumstances were beginning to sort themselves out in her mind. All the questions she had been asking herself, even those she hadn't thought to ask, were finding their answers here. The pieces of the puzzle were beginning to fall into place.

Jeremy's violent dislike for the manager, the sarcasm in Leon's tone when he had referred to Jeremy as "perfect", was now explained. How could she have missed it? Certainly there had been an abundance of clues, and what Leon had said during their last conversation finally made sense in the light of what she had just learned. Ida's seducer—Leon's rival—was none other than Jeremy. Having decided to marry Marion, he had put an end to his relationship with Ida. Had, in fact, abandoned her even though she was pregnant. So Ida had tried to convince Jeremy to marry her and the word "duty" in her note revealed a reason that made her demand unmistakably valid. But she had not returned from the meeting with Jeremy near the Green Pond.

"How did you get this note?" Marion whispered, her voice choked with feeling.

"We found it in the clothes we picked up to be mended—in Isabel's clothes."

"Isabel's clothes?" Marion repeated in amazement. That was strange. "When?"

"The day before you came back," Marguerite said. "We thought of going to the police . . . but we weren't sure what to do. We didn't want to hurt you. But now, after what you said, we knew you had to know."

Marion nodded, her face white. "Do you think Jeremy . . . ?"

Marguerite looked away, unable to respond to Marion's question. Timidly, Beth glanced up.

"We don't know," she answered in a quiet voice. "Maybe," she added, her voice merely a whisper.

"Yes . . . maybe," Marion repeated.

That the elegant, urbane Jeremy, as beautiful as an

archangel, could be behind something as sordid and tragic as this seemed impossible to believe. Marion shuddered. The cold, unfeeling look in his eyes....Might he be able to...? Why? For her? It didn't make sense. Jeremy's uneasiness, his determination to have Leon convicted now took on another meaning. Leon was the perfect suspect, having been Ida's rejected lover.

Did Jeremy kill Ida, she kept asking herself.

Marguerite and Beth stared at her with compassion. Even though Marion had not spoken aloud, her question seemed to reverberate through the room.

Chapter 15

Tiger jumped onto Marion's bed and settled down with his paws curled under him, looking very much like a sphinx. Marion stood by the window, the note Marguerite and Beth had given her only an hour before in her hand. She felt stunned, drained. She ached to sleep but her tormented thoughts had forced her to her feet. Suddenly the silence in the room was shattered by a brisk knock on the door.

"Darling?"

It was Jeremy. Marion felt a shiver go through her body.

"May I come in?"

After some hesitation she slipped the note under her mattress and replied, in as calm a voice as she could manage, "Yes. Come in."

The door opened and Jeremy walked into the room, as handsome as ever in a dark tweed suit and a light blue shirt that brought out the color of his eyes. The sun glistened on his blond hair. Full of self-confidence, he strode toward Marion who stood motionless by the window. "I've come to apologize," he said. He leaned forward to kiss her, but she turned her face away in an abrupt movement.

"Still angry? Don't you want to kiss your future husband?"

His slight frown changed to an indulgent smile. "You must be very nervous. Well, that's quite understandable."

Marion turned to face him, giving him a cold stare. She knew what she had to do. "I am nervous," she said flatly. "And with good reason."

He did not appear concerned. When he spoke his voice was calm and carefully modulated. "What is it? Is something bothering you?"

"I've seen the note Ida wrote you, asking to meet you at the Green Pond."

Jeremy turned white. "What note?" he asked, unable to mask a slight trembling in his voice. His nervousness made it clear to Marion that he knew what she was referring to.

"What note?" he demanded a second time, his voice threatening. "I don't know what you are talking about."

"It doesn't matter whether you'll admit to knowing about it or not," Marion continued in a confident voice. Inside she was terrified. "What does matter is what the note said...and what it means. You're not going to try to deny that you and Ida were having an affair, are you?"

Jeremy's face was wet with perspiration and he looked tense and guarded, no longer the casual man of elegance.

"Admit it," Marion said coldly, amazed that she could say what she heard herself saying. "You had an affair with Ida Somers. This letter said so very clearly."

"Show me this letter," Jeremy commanded as he sat down abruptly on the love seat.

"I can't," Marion responded. Her heart was racing. She wasn't sure what to expect, or how Jeremy would respond. She held her breath. "I gave it to the police."

"You what?" Jeremy shouted, jumping to his feet. "You'd better be lying, Marion, because if you're not, you will regret it." His voice was cold and menacing. "Tell me you're lying, Marion."

"It's true. The police have it. If you never received it, why should you care? You don't even know what it says."

Jeremy sank into the love seat. With an effort he regained control of himself. "What did this note say?"

"That you were having an affair with Ida. That you were the father of her child. And that she wanted you to meet her at the Green Pond."

"Marion—did you *really* give that note to the police?"

Marion trembled. She couldn't bear to see the expression on Jeremy's face. Was he guilty of murdering Ida? She *had* to know.

"Yes, I did," she continued boldly, wincing with the effort to keep up the pretense.

"Don't you see what this will do to me? How could you have done that? Even if I am innocent—and, believe me, I *am*—I'll have a very hard time proving it."

"But you can't be innocent," Marion replied sarcastically.

Jeremy looked away with embarrassment. "Yes, Marion, I did have an affair with Ida. But I did not murder her. You must believe me. I can see why that letter would upset you—maybe even make you want to call off the wedding. But please, listen to me.

"It all happened long before I even met you. Ida threw herself at me. Call it what you will, whatever we had together was of little importance to me, but Ida wanted more—she wanted to get married."

Jeremy seemed to have lost every vestige of his usual arrogance as he struggled to find the right thing to say. He was even having trouble pronouncing words properly. They tumbled out of his mouth in a rush. "It was never my intention to marry her. When I met you, I told Ida that it was all over. But she had just found out that she was pregnant. S-she was determined that I would marry her and she started pestering me. That's why I finally had to fire her."

And then, as though to excuse himself, he added, "Many men have found themselves in the same unfortunate position...."

Marion ignored his last words. "In her letter," she continued, "Ida seemed to be threatening you with a scandal, so it sure looks like you might have wanted to—"

"No!" Jeremy cried, his voice harsh. He took a handkerchief from his pocket and slowly wiped the perspiration from his face. But when he spoke, his voice was much calmer. "I did not kill Ida, Marion. I didn't go to meet her. In fact I didn't know anything about this meeting at the Green Pond. I may have made some very stupid mistakes, but I've certainly never killed anyone."

Marion began to cry. It did seem unbelievable that Jeremy, handsome elegant Jeremy, could be capable of such a sordid crime. His denial seemed sincere. Marion didn't love Jeremy anymore, but he was the man she had agreed to marry and she wanted to believe in his innocence. "This letter would seem to prove the contrary."

"But I never got the letter."

"Yet you don't deny knowing what was in it."

Again he looked away. No longer was he the confident Jeremy, always so sure of himself. Suddenly he looked panic-stricken and he was trembling visibly.

"Ida said in the letter that she intended to come to the château and give it to someone who would hand it to you personally," Marion said. "It seems quite logical to assume that it must have reached you."

Jeremy's voice wavered as he continued in his own defense. "All I can say is that I never went to meet Ida. You must believe me. But what's the use. The police will be here soon, and...." Jeremy's words trailed off and he dropped his head into his hands in a gesture of despair.

Marion raised a hand to her forehead. She did not enjoy playing the role of accuser. "I don't know what to think, anymore, Jeremy. But I must tell you something.

I lied. . .I—I burned it. I had to find out how you would react. I'm sorry. I did not take the letter to the police."

Jeremy raised his head slowly and stared at Marion, his eyes cold and penetrating.

At that moment the door, which had been left partly ajar, was pushed wide open and Isabel walked into the room. She closed the door behind her and spoke in the authoritarian voice she sometimes used. "What's going on? I was in my room and I thought I could hear arguing."

"Isabel, please leave," Jeremy ordered. "Marion and I will work this out ourselves."

Marion looked at Jeremy with surprise. He was usually quite solicitous of Isabel. Marion had never seen him get angry or impatient with her, no matter how irritating she might be.

Obediently, Isabel turned to go.

"Stay, Isabel," Marion called out on an impulse. She wasn't getting anywhere with Jeremy. Nothing he said gave her any more information that she had already. Perhaps Isabel would be able to provide a clue.

"No, Marion," Jeremy said loudly, "Isabel will go." He glared at his cousin and nodded toward the door as if to say *go*.

"Isabel," Marion interrupted. "What do you know about the note to Jeremy from Ida?"

"The note?" Isabel turned from the door, her carefully made-up face a perfectly controlled mask. "What note?"

"Go back to your room, Isabel. Marion doesn't know what she is talking—"

"You're lying. Isabel—you know what note I mean. The note telling Jeremy to meet Ida at the Green Pond."

"The note! Jeremy! What are we going to do?"

Marion tensed. So Isabel did know something, but what?

"Isabel," Jeremy spoke up. "Marion is quite upset. She knows, now, that I had an affair with Ida. But I think we can deal with that. What is more upsetting,

I'm sure you'll regret to hear, is that she thinks I murdered Ida." Jeremy paused, staring intently at his cousin. "Do you understand what that would mean? She would call off the wedding."

Isabel started, her face suddenly white. "No, Marion. You—you must not do that."

Marion stared at her. She couldn't understand what had just happened. She couldn't understand why, in the face of all that was going on, Jeremy and Isabel were saying what they were saying. Were they crazy?

"So you see, Isabel," Jeremy went on, his voice deep with meaning, "she must be shown that I didn't do it. *You* must tell her what really happened."

"*Me?*" Isabel asked, with a puzzled frown.

"Yes, Isabel. You. Go ahead," he urged her. "After the wedding, I will look after you. I will make sure that nothing will harm you. Go ahead," he went on, his voice a hypnotic lull, "tell her what happened at the Green Pond."

Isabel sank into a chair, her eyes fixed on Jeremy. "At the Green Pond? But—"

"You must, Isabel. Tell her what happened to Ida when you went to the pond."

Marion shivered with revulsion. Had Isabel strangled Ida? How was that possible? She thought of Isabel's history of mental upset. She thought of the strange fact that the note had been found folded away in Isabel's mending. Did this explain it?

"He's telling you the truth," confirmed Isabel suddenly, smiling at Jeremy. "Ida handed me that letter, herself and asked me to give it to Jeremy."

After a brief pause she took a deep breath and continued with a dramatic sigh.

"Naturally I opened it and read it. I knew what kind of a girl Ida was and poor Jeremy would never have been able to defend himself against her. So I went to the Green Pond to meet her. She was there, dressed in that red dress, looking like some kind of a devil. She was furious because Jeremy hadn't come and started to insult me. At one point, she actually threatened me."

The old woman's insane laughter filled the room. A shudder passed through Marion's body.

"She started to come toward me," Isabel continued dreamily, "and she raised her hand as though to strike me. I just . . . reached out and grabbed her by the throat. She struggled . . . but not for long."

"So . . . it was you . . ." Marion whispered. Stunned, she stared at Isabel's large, bony hands. Were these the hands that had wrapped themselves around Ida's slender neck? And committing her horrible crime, had Jeremy's cousin quietly walked back to the château and had her dinner with the rest of the family? She now appeared every inch a female version of Jekyll and Hyde. Outside the window the same white butterflies darted in the sunlight, the same birds were singing of spring and the same sweet scent of flowers filled the air. The sun was still shining, the sky was still blue. Everything seemed peaceful. The world does not change because one person dies, Marion realized, or because horror comes into the lives of a few.

In a hard, unfeeling voice Isabel continued. "Anyway . . . it was the only solution! That damn girl never would have left us alone. Good riddance. I say she got exactly what she deserved."

She was speaking about the murder as if it were a normal, logical act. Ida was an embarrassment to Jeremy, so she had to be eliminated. In the same calm tone she added, "You can be very sure that I wasn't going to let a girl like that interfere with our plans."

On more than one occasion Marion had noticed that Isabel seemed quite obsessed with the notion that nothing must happen to prevent the marriage between she and Jeremy. And yet Marion was quite aware that Isabel had no particular affection for her.

In the confident tone of a person who is quite sure she is acting in the best interests of everyone concerned, Isabel went on. "Jeremy knew nothing about the arrangements Ida had made to meet him. It was not until later, when that girl's body was found, that I told him everything so we could at least act accordingly."

Marion was shaking with indignation. "And you agreed to let an innocent man be accused!" she said in a voice that trembled.

"Altamira?" Isabel shrugged. "So what? I've never liked that man, anyway. And after all, he got out of it, didn't he? Now the whole thing will be forgotten soon and no one will ever speak of it again. If I hadn't lost that letter, you wouldn't have known anything about what actually happened."

Marion felt herself swaying. She felt quite ill and thought she was going to faint. To steady herself, she leaned against the dresser.

Meanwhile, Jeremy appeared to have regained his self-confidence. "Well, Marion, now you know.... I didn't kill Ida, and I couldn't accuse Isabel. She's my cousin. She practically raised me. Besides, she has a problem....I'll explain it to you later," he said softly, glancing toward Isabel, who had casually lighted a cigarette and was staring into space with a pleased, glazed expression on her face. "Besides, she was threatened and insulted by that girl and got carried away in a moment of anger. You could even call it an accident. Certainly, she was acting in self-defense."

He was absolving Isabel, while not having a single feeling of compassion for the unfortunate victim. Marion felt pity for the poor woman who had left not even the suggestion of regret in the heart of the man she had loved. "You may not have killed Ida, Jeremy," she said. "Your guilt is of quite a different nature. You wished for this crime and then learned of it having happened, which makes you something of an accomplice—albeit after the fact. To protect Isabel you accused an innocent man."

Leon had almost had to pay the ultimate price for a crime he did not commit because of this conspiracy of silence. This was what she would never be able to forgive.

"There are too many lies. Too much hypocrisy," she said. "I can't marry you, Jeremy. It's quite impossible."

She might have married Jeremy out of respect for a promise, believing him to be loyal and above reproach. Now she knew he was neither. Now she knew that the magnificent facade, the impeccable manners, hid treachery and moral weakness. This discovery finally severed the only remaining link with him.

"Marion," Jeremy said, "you can't be serious. I didn't know what Isabel had done until just a while ago.... Late last night, in fact. I thought Altamira was guilty. We can't just call everything off three days before the wedding. Think of the consequences ... the scandal."

She lowered her head. Was he telling the truth? Those noises she had heard in the night—had it been Isabel going to talk to Jeremy? And even if not, did it matter anymore?

"I have thought about all that, Jeremy."

"Well, you can't do it!" he insisted emphatically. "Think of my mother. Can't you imagine how she's going to feel...how hurt she'll be? She might even have an attack."

"I wish there was some way I might have spared her," said Marion in a voice very close to breaking.

When she lifted her head her eyes were filled with tears. She was unable to express her own hurt at having to cause this noble woman such pain.

"My mother has become very fond of you," Jeremy was saying. "Even if it were only for her sake, couldn't you—"

"Don't, Jeremy....No matter how embarrassing, how painful it may prove to be, my decision is—"

"But you can't make a decision just like that. You need a little time to think about it. With time," Jeremy persisted, "I'm sure I could earn your forgiveness."

He still believed in the power of his charm. His voice was soft and caressing as he continued. "Marion, don't let this unfortunate incident destroy our whole future...the happiness that lies ahead for us. Before very long, we'll have forgotten all this. It will seem like a bad dream that goes away in the morning sun. I didn't kill Ida. You know that. The only thing for which you could possibly hold me responsible is having had an affair with her. How many men are there, anywhere, who could boast that they had not had such an affair?"

"It isn't the fact that you had an affair with Ida," sighed Marion. "Or that you abandoned her when you should have been able to face up to your responsibilities toward her. It's the lies, Jeremy, the treachery, that I can't forgive."

"If I seem to have acted badly, it was only because of my love for you. I was afraid that I might lose you."

Marion shook her head. She had never been sure of his love for her and, even at this very moment, when he was telling her that he loved her, his eyes held no warmth. And yet she should have been convinced. Otherwise why would he want to marry her? She wondered if he was capable of loving anyone. Now everything about him seemed false and artificial.

"I can understand your revulsion at being mixed up in all of this. I did everything I could to keep you out of it. I beg of you, Marion, don't let yourself be carried away by your anger and resentment toward me. You're in shock right now. After you've had a little time to think about it, you'll see things in a different light. Surely you're not going to sacrifice our happiness merely on an impulse."

He did not know that she had stopped loving him, that the enchantment simply wasn't there for her anymore. She looked at him with deep sadness. Although she might have been mistaken in believing that she had loved him, he was still her first dream.

"Jeremy, I'm sorry, but...."

Isabel, who had been lost in her own thoughts until now, spoke up. "What are you saying? You don't want to marry Jeremy?"

Her tone was menacing, her lips drew back from her

teeth, and her eyes glittered. Was this the way she had looked when she strangled Ida near the Green Pond?

"That will be enough, Isabel," Jeremy said sharply.

"But we can't give up. Not now when we've almost reached our goal."

He reached out and grabbed her arm. "For God's sake, shut up! Nothing is lost. Marion is upset, that's all. She'll get over it." Then, he turned to Marion. "Isabel is very concerned about our happiness, darling."

He smiled tenderly. "I'm sure you don't want me to be unhappy either, do you, Marion?" he murmured.

Even though she was shaking her head, he still hoped that with a lot of tact and some fancy maneuvering, everything would fall into place, the way he wanted.

"I must rest," Marion pleaded in a soft voice. "Please leave. I need to think."

"Marion—how do we know that you...you won't do something rash?" Jeremy asked.

Isabel had risen from her chair and was pacing the room. "Jeremy, she could call the police. Now she knows too much. What's going to happen?"

"Be quiet, Isabel. I can handle this," Jermy insisted impatiently.

"I won't call the police, Isabel," Marion stated grimly, "if that's what you're worried about. It might kill Martha," she added in a barely audible voice.

It was true. Marion didn't know what to do, who to turn to. She wanted to talk to Leon, but she was beginning to fear that Jeremy and Isabel might not let her out of their sight.

"I can't believe *you*," Isabel said viciously. "I don't know about you, Jeremy, but I'm staying here. Your previous fiancée can get all the rest she needs. I won't stop her."

"Isabel, I told you to be quiet," Jeremy said, his voice rising.

"Well, whose innocent neck is it, anyway?"

Marion stood, watching first one and then the other. The atmosphere was sickeningly charged. She couldn't

understand the meaning behind what was being said
and there was no telling what could happen. What was
clear, however, was that she wasn't going to be able to
get away. Unless. . . .

Chapter 16

Marion knew suddenly that she was going to have to gain Jeremy's trust, and the only way to do that would be to convince him that she *was* going to marry him, that she still loved him. She held her breath before she spoke. "Isabel, I must say something in private to Jeremy. Do you mind leaving the room?"

"What do you have to say that can't be said in front of me?" Isabel asked suspiciously.

"Isabel, leave," Jeremy ordered.

As soon as they were alone Marion began. "Jeremy, I—I'm sorry for having been so wrong about you. I want you to know that I do...love you and want to marry you."

Jeremy looked at her coldly for a long moment. With a sinking heart, Marion knew that he wasn't convinced, that she would have to work harder. "I'm sorry about all the things I said," she went on. "I was angry. I didn't know what to think! And that note—it surprised me so much. I thought everything was lost, and I couldn't stand the thought of that. Can you understand, darling?" she asked, reaching out to take his hand. "Please," she went on, standing in front of him, "say everything will be all right."

Jeremy only looked at her steadily. "Kiss me," he demanded, pulling her roughly into his arms. His mouth covered hers with a crushing kiss. Marion stifled back her anger and revulsion and tried desperately to respond amorously.

He released her finally, his smile indicating that he had been satisfied. "I'm relieved, Marion, but promise me that you won't tell anyone what happened here. The results could be devastating, I don't have to tell you that."

"I promise, Jeremy," Marion said, looking into his eyes, hoping that there would be no sign of what she was really thinking, no indication of the nausea she felt, the tumultuous swirling feeling in her head. "I wouldn't want to hurt my own family would I?"

"Very well then. I believe you," he finally said, breaking away to go to the door to tell Isabel.

Marion could hear Isabel's plaintive voice. For a moment it sounded as if she wasn't going to go along with Jeremy, but then there was some mention of the wedding and she quieted down, her footsteps echoing in the hall.

Jeremy came back into the room, relief evident on his face. "Well," he said, "dinner will be served shortly and I need to wash up. Now that everything is taken care of, do you mind?"

"No—not at all," Marion responded, hoping that she didn't sound too eager. "I want to rest."

As soon as he was gone she went to her desk and took out a note and pen. She paused only for a moment before writing.

Dear Leon, I must see you tonight. I have important information. Can you meet me at the teahouse? I will try to be there at midnight.

She signed her name, wondering who she could give the note to. She didn't dare take the path to Leon's house in daylight for fear that she might be seen. She dreaded the thought of going through the forest alone at night, but she had no other choice. Jeremy wouldn't be going to work the next day, and she could only really slip away after everyone else had gone to bed.

Just then there was a knock at the door. Marion hurriedly slipped the piece of paper into the desk. "Come in," she said as calmly as she could.

Jeanne, the young maid, appeared in the doorway. "Dinner is served, Miss Charles."

"Oh—thank you Jeanne. I had forgotten the time." Marion rose to her feet. "Tell me, isn't there someone who delivers wood to the kitchen every evening?" Marion had noticed on a few occasions a strong young man carrying load after load of kindling to the kitchen each evening around this time.

"You mean Tom?"

"I guess so." Now Marion knew his name, but she didn't know how she might get the note to him. "Jeanne, can you keep a secret? I'd like to give Tom a note to take to Leon Altamira. If I give it to you to give to him, and if you don't tell a soul about it, I'll give you one of my new dresses from Paris—whichever one you like."

Jeanne cried out. "Miss Charles, do you mean it? Of course—and I promise I won't tell."

Marion went to the desk and drew out the note, slipped it into an envelope, sealed it and gave it to Jeanne. "Remember—if I find out that you told anyone, you won't get the dress. And please tell Tom that I will give him ten dollars if he keeps his end of the bargain. Just be sure that Leon gets the note tonight, understand?"

"Yes, Miss Charles, I understand. Thank you!" Jeanne took the note and slipped out of the room.

It was out of Marion's hands now. She could only hope that they would be honest enough to do as they were asked.

Quickly she washed and changed for dinner and descended the stairs with a sinking feeling in her stomach. She would have to continue her "performance," convincing Jeremy and Isabel that they could trust her. Later she would meet Leon and tell him everything.

IT TOOK FOREVER. Marion was relieved that Jeremy retired early for the evening. By ten, all was quiet. Marion went to her room and tried to rest. She took a long, bubbly, fragrant bath. She tried to read a book, but it was no use—she was too excited about meeting Leon. It was all she could think of.

At eleven-thirty, she began to get ready. The evening was much chillier than the day and she would have to dress warmly. Finally it was time to go. She noted with thanks that the moon was full. She would be able to find her way along the path without too much difficulty. She was frightened. What if someone saw her? What would it be like in the forest all by herself? What would she do if a wolf crossed the path?

As quickly as she could she slipped through her door and into the hall, wincing at the loud squeaking of the floorboards. She held her breath and froze. Had she heard someone moving in one of the rooms? Her pulse was pounding in her ears. It must have been something else. She had to get out—to the teahouse, to Leon. She started down the stairs and in no time at all was easing her way through the massive front doors. She left one slightly ajar; she didn't want to get locked out.

She paused for a moment outside in the archway over the door. Here, she knew, she could not be seen from the house. She spotted the opening to the path she wanted across the clearing. Now she regretted that the moon was bright. She couldn't risk being seen. She studied the sky—there were a few clouds. If she waited a few minutes, one of them might cross in front of the moon, affording her a second's hiding. In that time she would be able to make a run across the grass for the path. She waited, her heart racing, listening to every sound in the forest, trembling to hear a lone wolf's howl across the valley. A wind came up and shook the trees, the rustling leaves filling the silent night with sound. It was beautiful—clear and sparkling. In spite of everything Marion thrilled to the wonder of it all, pulling her sweater closer around her to ward off the chilly, spring night air.

Suddenly it was dark. Marion bolted for the path, racing across the clearing. It seemed to take forever; she could imagine millions of pairs of eyes following her from the many windows of the château. She felt less vulnerable, more protected when she reached the forest edge, but once she started along the lonely path through the dark, thick woods, she grew more and more frightened. The terrifying image of Ida, struggling in a lost battle for her life, kept coming back to her. It must have been on a night such as this one, in woods such as these that she was attacked. She, too, must have been scared of the night, of the woods, and to have been attacked by Isabel and to have known, if only for a moment before everything went black, that all was lost, that her life was at stake. Could it be true? Could Isabel have actually murdered Ida? Did she have the strength, even, to overcome a young, struggling woman? Marion shook her head as she walked quickly along. It hardly seemed possible.

Before long Marion came to the big boulder where she had put her clothes the day she had seen Leon. Marion smiled. Soon she would be with him—soon she would have comfort. She knew the teahouse would not be too far ahead.

The little wood bridge over the stream came into view. Marion crossed it eagerly, making out the posts and the walls of the teahouse in the moonlit night. She saw the shadow of a man inside, standing against the post. She saw the shape of the familiar hat Leon sometimes wore.

"Leon," she cried out, and ran up the steps to the entrance.

The man's back was to her. He turned around. She ran to him eagerly, breathless with fear of the night and the thrill of seeing him again.

Marion stopped suddenly, rooted to the spot. Something was wrong...it wasn't Leon. Who was it? She looked into the man's face and screamed. It was Jeremy, and the ice cold glint in his eyes and the hard line of his lips told her that he wasn't the Jeremy she knew.

"Jeremy—please—no—you don't understand," she stuttered, backing away as he approached her. With one easy reach he grabbed her, his hands encircling her neck, hard, in a way that told her that her life, too, was endangered.

Marion panicked. She tried to scream again, but no sound came out. "Don't, Jeremy, please," she begged. "Leon...coming."

"You are wrong, Marion, darling. Leon will not be coming. The police will think it was he, however. They will have the note you so thoughtfully wrote him minutes after you had sworn your love for me, a note that you will be happy to hear will hang him."

Tears sprang to Marion's eyes and she tried struggling against him, scratching him, kicking him, fighting for her very life, but it was useless. She could feel herself shaking from head to toe. She felt nauseous, helpless. His hands were around her neck. There was nothing she could do. "You...killed Ida," Marion gasped.

Jeremy answered with a laugh. "Yes, of course it was me. And I learned how easy it can be."

His fingers tightened and Marion began to black out. She fought for air desperately, convulsions overcoming her in her struggle. Suddenly she felt Jeremy's hands fly from her neck. She fell to the floor, hearing, as if from another world, the sounds of a fight. Terrified, she gathered the strength to raise her head. It was Leon, and he had Jeremy pinned to the post. Several strong punches, and Jeremy slumped to the floor, unconscious.

Leon leaped to Marion and took her in his arms. She was limp and faint. The air she had so desperately fought for was slow in coming. Then, as her breathing gradually returned to normal the realization of what had just happened came to her, and cradled in Leon's strong, protective arms, she gave in to deep, racking sobs.

"Oh, my love, I was almost too late," he said softly. "The police insisted on coming with me. I was to meet them on the other side of the path, but they never showed up."

Several spotlights in the woods and loud crashing noises indicated that they had finally made it. "Officer! Over here," Leon yelled. The two police officers cautiously approached the teahouse, their guns drawn. "It's okay, he's out cold."

"What happened?" the young officer asked, alarmed to see Marion's tear-streaked, pale and frightened face.

"He tried...he tried to kill her," was all Leon could say. Tenderly he tilted Marion's chin to examine her neck. "You will have bruises for a while, Marion. They will go away. But in your heart—that bruise may take forever to heal," he said gently, understanding fully the horror she had just experienced.

She smiled and looked into his eyes. She loved him with all her being. Still faint and shaking, she let her head sink against his chest. Leon caressed her cheek and the soft curls of her hair. "Do you think you could look after him?" Leon called out to the officers who were handcuffing Jeremy's barely unconscious body.

"No problem. We'd like to take him to the station tonight."

"I think that would be best. I'm going to take Marion back to the château now. Will it be all right if she doesn't testify until tomorrow?"

"No. I'm afraid we will have to talk to her tonight—if she is able."

"Well...okay, but could you call for a doctor to come to the château? I'd like him to look at Marion and I'm concerned about Mrs. Koster when she finds out. I don't want to take any chances."

Leon turned and lifted Marion effortlessly in his

arms. "Are you comfortable?" he asked with a smile.

She didn't speak, but answered by resting her head on his wide shoulder. She sighed deeply and relaxed in his arms. His suede jacket smelled good, like the outdoors. She knew she was safe now, that everything would be all right. Lulled by his steady walk along the moonlit path, she drifted into sleep.

Chapter 17

There were no lights on in the château. Leon was glad—he wanted to keep the events of the evening secret until the police and the doctor arrived.

Marion raised her head and looked around. The towering walls of the château glimmered in the cool moonlight. "I left the door open," she said in a sleepy voice. "We can go right in."

Leon slipped in the door and down the hall until he came to Marguerite's door. After a moment he heard a noise within. "Who is it?" a timid, high voice inquired, edged with fear.

"Leon," he said softly, hoping no one else in the servants' quarters would hear, "and Marion."

Immediately the door opened onto the warm cheery room. "Oh, my goodness," Marguerite gasped when she saw Marion in Leon's arms. She scurried to the sofa to clear off the piles of magazines and sewing and embroidery notions that invariably covered it. "Put her here," she said and hurried into the other room, returning with a pile of soft, patchwork quilts and a pillow. She tucked the pillow under Marion's head, blanching at the frightening sight of great red welts on Marion's neck.

"Oh, no!" she gasped, looking up at Leon. "Did...?"

Leon merely nodded gravely. "He's been taken to the police station."

Marguerite covered Marion with a quilt and sat down beside her. Marion opened her eyes and smiled, tears coming to her eyes. "Now, now, my poor dear," Marguerite said with loving concern. "You're not to think of anything. I'm going to put on the kettle to make tea. That's just what we all need."

"Marguerite," Leon interrupted. "What's the best way to let the police and the doctor know how to find us?"

"Leave a note on the door," she said after a moment's thought. "Tell them to come around to the door on the northeast corner," she added, getting a pen and note pad for Leon to write on. "Could you wake Beth up and tell her to come here on your way?" Leon nodded to them both and left.

Soon a brisk tapping on the door signaled Beth's entrance. She popped her head in apprehensively. "Leon told me," she said as Marguerite was about to fill her in. "Marion, dear. Goodness—you know, we never in a million years thought...."

Soon Leon was back, and the four sat and sipped their tea. Marguerite started a fire in the stove in the corner, and soon its crackling warmth and flickering light filled the room.

Their peaceful interlude was soon interrupted by an officious knock on the outside door. Leon jumped up to let in the two police officers, followed by the village doctor.

"You're in fine shape," the doctor pronounced. "I could give you a tranquilizer, if you wish, but you don't seem to need one."

Marion shook her head. "I'm okay," she said, and, with a signal from the doctor, Leon and the police gathered around.

Bit by bit, Marion told her story, starting with the note Marguerite and Beth had shown her earlier that day. Everyone in the room was silent as she described, often fighting back tears and holding Leon's hand for comfort, how Jeremy had tried to strangle her. There were no questions—only a stunned silence. Then Leon began, explaining how he had pulled Jeremy off Marion.

"How did Jeremy know I was going to be there?" Marion asked, sitting up. "And how did you know to call the police and come for me?" she asked Leon, expressing a question that had been plaguing her for a while.

Marguerite spoke up. "That's where we come in. Jeanne gave your note to Tom, just as you asked, but Tom opened it, and decided that there would be more money in it for him if he showed the note to Jeremy— for a price, of course. True enough, Jeremy gave him a hundred dollars for the note, without even seeing it. It was then that Tom started to worry about what he had done. He's greedy, but not a bad boy, so he came to me and Beth to ask our advice. That's when we got frightened. We wrote a letter to Leon, explaining it all to him, and made Tom run it down to Leon's house right away. Leon sent Tom for the police."

"I couldn't use the phone, you see," Leon interjected, "because all the lines around here are party lines and someone at the château might have listened in." He turned to the officers. "Why were you late meeting me?"

The young officer grimaced and shook his head. "We got lost in the woods," he said sheepishly, and they all smiled in spite of the tragic consequences that may have been the result of such a simple human mistake.

"Where is Jeremy now?" Marion asked with a trembling voice.

"He's at the station. He's been charged with murder and attempted murder. I don't think he will be getting out for many years to come—if ever."

Marion lowered her head to hide the tears in her eyes. It seemed so unreal, so unbelievable. She could still remember their enchanted evenings together in Paris, and how she had loved him—or believed that she had loved him.

Had it all been false? Had he never loved her? Why had he wanted to marry her? Their marriage had been so important to him that he had killed for her. Why? There were still so many questions.

"I don't understand," Marion sighed. "What about Isabel? Why did she want me to think that she killed Ida?"

"I think I know the answer to that," Leon said softly, "but I'd like it to wait for the morning when we talk to Mrs. Koster. Doctor, could you stay until the morning? I'm worried about alarming Martha Koster by waking her."

"I don't think you'll have that luxury, Mr. Altamira," the older officer with the mustache spoke up. "I'm afraid the news reporters will get wind of this. You're apt to be getting visitors and phone calls soon. I'm surprised the news hounds haven't picked up the trail already."

Leon nodded gravely. "Very well then, we'll have to tell her now. Marion...could you? She would be less startled by you than by any of us. We'll be outside the door and as soon as you call us in, we'll be there."

Marion nodded. Gingerly she sat up and got to her feet. She still felt faint, but she knew that now the cause was emotional more than anything else. With resolve she knew she could do it. Thinking about the welfare of someone she loved strengthened her, taking her mind from her own troubles. Gravely, she, Leon and the doctor left the room, knowing that the hardest challenge of the night was still to come.

Timidly, Marion knocked on the door to Martha Koster's suite of rooms on the ground floor. Silence reigned. She knocked again. After a moment they could hear faint noises and a frail call of, "Who is it?" Marion answered and slipped into the room. "Martha," Marion began, not knowing quite what to say. "Something has happened, but I don't want you to get upset. Leon and the doctor are here. Can I ask them in to talk to you?"

"What? What is it all about, Marion? Tell me," Martha insisted anxiously.

"I . . . can't, Martha. I want Leon to explain it. Please, say it's all right for them to come in."

Martha Koster thought for a moment, her face white with tension. "Yes, if you insist."

Relieved, Marion went to the door and admitted Leon and the doctor. The three pulled chairs around Martha's bed, where the frail old woman looked at them all expectantly.

Leon cleared his throat and began. "This story goes back many years," he began. "To the last century, in fact. At that time, the emperor, Napoleon the Third, sent troops to Mexico to assist Maximilian of Austria gain the throne there and at the same time defend the throne against Juarez, the former president of the republic. It was wild and dangerous in that country. The soldiers were hated by some and loved by others. They were the antiguerrillas, fighting courageously among the soldiers of the antiguerrilla movement and despite many wounds received in ambushes, Maximilian was one of the few survivors of that heroic adventure. In the long run, it served no real purpose, but it was a time of supreme bravery."

Marion and the doctor looked at Leon with curiosity. Marion couldn't understand why Leon was telling this story—now, of all times. Martha Koster didn't seem confused by it at all, however—her face was radiant with emotion. "Yes, you are right," she nodded, "and we know that Ludovic of Spain returned to Paris, married and then died, without ever having any children. At least that's what my researchers have told me."

"That's true, but not the whole truth, Mrs. Koster. During one of the skirmishes, he was wounded and taken to a small village called Altamira, where he was treated. The village was named after the Spanish family that founded it. Anti-Juariste, the Altamira family took him in and cared for him with great devotion."

He paused and looked around the room before continuing. "Even during the worst moments of war," he resumed, "love may still bloom. Such a love did, indeed, bloom between Ludovic and the daughter of the household, the beautiful Pilar. A Catholic priest blessed their union and a child was born, a baby girl they named Dolores. The baby's mother died giving birth."

The silence in the room was broken only by the howl of a wolf in the hills. Immediately it was answered by another as Leon went on. "When Napoleon called back his troops to France, the guerrilla movement executed Maximilian and the Juaristes took over power. Ludovic returned to Paris and married, leaving the small Dolores in the care of her maternal family. He never went back to Altamira. However he did write several times, asking for news and even set up a trust for her. When she came of age, Dolores married one of her second cousins, Manuel Altamira." After a brief pause he added softly, "Dolores was my grandmother."

"Leon, d-do you mean...?" Martha Koster stammered, reaching her hand out to him. "If what you say is true, you...you are a descendant of the princes of Sayn. How do you know all this, Leon?"

Marion had been hanging on Leon's every word. She didn't doubt that Leon was telling the truth, and that along with the blood of beautiful Pilar, the noble blood of the Sayn family ran in his veins. With a start she remembered Mrs. Martineau's recollection of Leon's striking resemblance to Mrs. Koster's cousin, handsome Leopold, who had been lost in a tragic plane crash.

"I have in my possession certain letters that Ludovic wrote to his daughter. But I have other proof of my origins," he added. He opened the collar of his shirt, baring his tanned, robust neck. Near the inside of his shoulder, where the skin was much lighter from having been protected from the sun, four small brown spots formed the shape of a cloverleaf.

"Truth," Martha Koster said quietly, "is sometimes

stranger than fiction. It's a beautiful story, Leon. I welcome you with all my heart."

"It's a birthmark peculiar to the Sayn family," Mrs. Koster explained to the others. "It appears on only some members of the family and not in every generation. I don't have such a birthmark, but my brother did and so did my granddaughter. It's irrefutable proof that what Leon is saying is the truth."

"But," cried Marion suddenly, "I have a birthmark exactly like that, and in the same place!"

"Yes," Leon said quietly. "You do."

"But what does it mean?" Marion asked. "I don't understand."

Softly Leon explained. "I saw that mark yesterday, and it was then that I understood. Your name is not Marion Charles. You are Josina Reinfeld, Mrs. Koster's granddaughter, the child who was believed drowned in the Green Pond."

There was absolute silence in the room. It seemed as if eveyone had stopped breathing.

"My God! Is it possible?" Mrs. Koster cried softly, her hands clasped in an attitude of prayer. Trembling she leaned toward Marion and gently reached to open the neck of her dress. Marion tensed. She didn't want Mrs. Koster to see the welts on her neck. She need not have worried, however, Martha Koster had only one thing in mind: the small flowerlike mark. "It's true," Martha Koster exclaimed, seeing the birthmark. "There can be no doubt. You are my little Josina. Oh, my God, all these years I've thought you were dead."

Slowly, Marion got to her feet and, as though in a trance, held out both her hands to Mrs. Koster. With incredible grace, the older woman took the young girl into her arms and held her close as both wept openly. It was a shock, of course, this revelation, but Martha Koster's tears were falling softly and there was not a sign of any physical distress. Her heartbeat, in fact, never had been steadier. After a few minutes the two managed to regain at least some of their composure, even laughing a little at each other as they wiped their eyes.

"But what could have happened?" Mrs. Koster asked finally.

"I think I can give you some idea of what really happened," Leon said.

Everyone was waiting to hear what was about to be said.

"I've spent some time going over the facts and finally was able to put a few things together. From all of this I think I can say I know at least some of the reasons behind it. Of course I don't pretend to know all the details, but I'm quite sure I can give you a general idea. Isabel," he said quietly, "is at the bottom of it all. She's the reason you've been deprived of your granddaughter's love for twenty years."

"Isabel?" repeated Mrs. Koster, astonished.

"Yes," Leon replied. "You see, it's a well-known fact that she was madly in love with your husband, Emile, who never showed the slightest interest in her. She came to hate you eventually, although she's always been able to hide her feelings. At some point her affection for Emile was transferred to his son Jeremy, and in time, it grew to be a kind of worship. Isabel always wanted Jeremy to have everything. Wealth, power, you name it, but she herself had nothing to give him. To say the least, she felt frustrated."

His tone was very respectful as he continued to speak. "When your daughter was killed in the car accident, Josina was left as your sole heir, and Isabel saw the perfect opportunity to assure Jeremy of your fortune. All she had to do was arrange for the disappearance of the only heir."

Mrs. Koster let out a small cry of disbelief as Leon went on.

"However she didn't kill the child. Perhaps she was unable to go quite that far. Instead she took advantage of the maid's momentary distraction and took your granddaughter away. Somehow she had Marion—that is, Josina—put into an orphanage. She must have thought that once your granddaughter was out of the way, you would make Jeremy the heir and master of your estate. It must have been very upsetting for her when it was finally discovered that even though you were very fond of Jeremy and have always been more than kind to him, you were unable to leave your fortune to anyone but the descendants of the princes of Sayn."

He paused to catch his breath before going on. "For some unknown reason, perhaps because he wasn't able to find an heiress wealthy enough for his taste, Jeremy, at thirty-eight, still remained unmarried. Then, I suspect that either Jeremy or Isabel came up with a new scheme. Find the lost child, marry her to Jeremy and then reveal her true identity. In his way Jeremy would ultimately become heir to the fortune, since part of the plan was that there would be no marriage contract. I am sure there's a private detective somewhere who has been paid a bundle to find the lost Josina. Well . . . we all know the rest."

Marion, who in fact was Josina, was listening intently, with a bitter taste in her mouth. She thought back to that rainy day in March when Jeremy had first come into the shop. She thought of all the things they had said to each other, their kisses and caresses. It had all seemed so enchanting. It had been a dream come true, and now she was learning that it had been a cold, calculating scheme. All the attention, the smiles, the compliments . . . everything had been part of the meticulous plan, engineered by Isabel and Jeremy. Jeremy had never loved her.

Jeremy had been the first man she had ever kissed, but for him the kiss had been nothing more than a maneuver. She had marveled at his generosity, while all the time he had been acting selfishly, thinking only of the fortune he stood to inherit. There wasn't a moment of joy to be found in any part of their relationship. It had all been treachery and lies. She felt abused. She felt sick to her stomach.

"It's so ugly," she murmured. She covered her face with her hands and wept.

Mrs. Koster gently put her hand on Marion's shoulder. "My poor child," she said softly.

Marion raised her head. "It was over anyway," she said bitterly. "I broke off my engagement to Jeremy because of his affair with Ida and the tragic death of that poor girl."

"Ida?" Mrs. Koster exclaimed. "What does Ida have to do with it?"

Leon and Marion glanced grimly at each other and then at the doctor. The time had come to tell Mrs. Koster the worst of the story.

"Mrs. Koster," the doctor said gently. "I'd like you to take your medication—"

"Why, what is it you are going to tell me?" Martha Koster demanded.

Marion took Martha's hand. "Grandmother," she said lovingly, bringing tears to both their eyes, "please, would you? We can't help but worry."

"You just hold my hand...Josina. I'll be all right."

Slowly, as carefully as he was able, Leon told the old woman about her stepson's affair with Ida—and how, in desperation, he had taken her life.

Leon nodded his head. "Poor Ida was upsetting his plans."

"My God!" Mrs. Koster exclaimed. "This is...." She stared at them all. "Jeremy...I loved him like a son."

Martha Koster bowed her head and wept. "I-I always knew there was something very...cold in Jeremy. I could never seem to reach his heart. I tried. Oh, I wanted to be close to him—but I just couldn't, I don't know why."

Marion moved closer to her new-found grandmother, wiping the tears from her own eyes.

"Where—where is he now?" Martha Koster asked.

"He's been arrested. He's at the police station," Leon stated. "Mrs. Koster, there is one more thing you have to know before the news is out."

Leon looked away, as if to collect his thoughts before he went on. "You should know that Jeremy has also been charged with...attempted murder."

"Attempted murder—of whom?" Martha Koster gasped.

"Marion," Leon said simply, looking steadily into her eyes.

"Marion?" Martha echoed, her voice failing, her emotions spent. "How? Why?" was all she said before she collapsed on the bed and the doctor moved to administer medication.

Chapter 18

In the spring days that followed, Martha Koster gradually recovered. Under Marion's care, in time she was back to normal health.

When informed of Jeremy's arrest, Isabel had confessed to the kidnapping and even tried to absolve Jeremy of any blame by insisting, sometimes violently, always insanely, that he had merely acted as she had bade him. Eventually she broke down completely and had to be taken to a psychiatric hospital where she would stay for the rest of her life.

Marion, who was gradually becoming accustomed to being called Josina, had at least one thing for which she could be thankful: there had been no wedding. The door that had been slowly closing on her future had suddenly been flung open to reveal a bright new road, at the end of which happiness was waiting. Although she still felt a little strange about it in many ways she was beginning to enjoy her new identity, which would soon be made official. All in all the days passed peacefully and a new kind of closeness developed between her and Martha Koster.

Every day Mrs. Koster marveled at the miracle that had returned her granddaughter to her. Often she would look at her, asking herself why she hadn't recognized Josina sooner, seeing in the young girl the reflection of so many of her own physical characteristics. Josina, of course, blossomed in the warmth of all this attention, much like a languishing plant that is suddenly placed in the sunlight.

Leon continued to live in his beautiful house in the clearing, having kept the duties of manager of the estate. But now he was welcomed to the château as a member of the family. Eventually he explained that having been made aware of his family origins at the time of his parent's death, he had begun a search for the place where his ancestors had settled. As soon as he graduated from the school of forestry he had answered an ad that Mrs. Koster had placed for someone to look after the estate. At first he was simply curious; then he had found that he loved the land, enjoyed working for Mrs. Koster and that he would be able to pursue his academic career at the same time. The situation was ideal.

When Mrs. Martineau learned of the true relationship between Leon and Mrs. Koster, she was triumphant, delighted to have been the first to see the resemblance between the handsome Leon and Leopold of Sayn, the love of her youth. Mrs. Martineau had more opportunity, now, to see them all. To fill the vacancy in the newly renovated wing, Martha Koster had invited her childhood friend to live there, an invitation that Julia Martineau accepted eagerly.

In the months that followed Leon often joined Mrs. Koster, Josina and Julia for lunch or dinner. On one such occasion, the day was particularly beautiful. The sky was blue as far as the eye could see and the warm, invigorating breeze coming from the mountains was filled with the scent of evergreen.

"Would you like to come for a walk, Josina?" he suggested after eveyone had finished their coffee and dessert.

"I'd love to," Josina beamed, her heart jumping. Although she and Leon had chances to see each other often, they were very rarely alone. Sometimes she wondered if Leon weren't allowing her to have a lot of time to herself—time to think, to cry, to get over the terrible shock.

Slowly they crossed the front lawn and headed toward the forest. From the window in the living room, where Martha and Julia sat knitting and chatting, Martha watched them go and smiled. She knew only too well the light of love when it lights a man's or woman's eyes, and she had seen such a light in the eyes of both Leon and Josina. "Oh, Julia, they are so beautiful together, don't you think?" she said wistfully. "And I do love them both."

Julia nodded with a nostalgic smile. "All our days will be happy ones now, my dear friend. You wait and see."

FOR A FEW MOMENTS the two young people walked in an emotionally charged silence. The green leaves and colorful flowers of summer were beginning to give way to the reds and browns of autumn. Leon looked at Josina. She had lost some weight over the past months and she looked even more graceful, more beautiful than ever. He took in the delicate wisps of dark hair encircling her angelic face, the long, slender neck, the smooth, white shoulders, and the proud bearing of her head.

Josina glanced at Leon nervously. Meeting his penetrating black eyes, her heart fluttered and she felt overwhelmed with feeling. Not knowing what to say or do, she said the first thing that came into her mind, stooping to pick a beautiful purple wild flower growing on the edge of the path.

"It's hard to imagine that we're cousins."

Leon smiled. "Oh—we're the kind of cousins that are so distant it doesn't really count," he said, catching her hand in his.

Josina stared at the suddenness of his touch. She looked at him, smiled and gently squeezed his hand. "But we *are* related."

"Oh, yes. That pretty little cloverleaf near your shoulder proves we're related. When I saw it, I realized who you were right away. And that's when it hit me that you were being used to guarantee Jeremy's future."

Leon saw Josina wince. "I'm sorry I said that," he whispered. "I promise I won't—ever again."

"No, Leon—we must talk about it. I need to talk about it. I keep wondering...what if I had married Jeremy, what then? What would have happened?"

"Yes," Leon said thoughtfully. "I can't help but wonder if Isabel would have gone so far as to kill Mrs. Koster—to revenge her marriage to Emile and to get what she wanted for Jeremy."

Josina recalled the expression on Isabel's face that time she gave Mrs. Koster her medication and realized that her plans might very well have included doing away with her benefactor. It would have been a simple matter to make sure that her pills were out of reach at any given time they might be needed.

"I'm inclined to agree with you," Josina said with a shudder. "Isabel must have been struggling for a long time. Envy and jealousy probably destroyed her judgment years ago, and Jeremy became an obsession with her. On top of that, I imagine that she wanted revenge against whoever she was blaming for her own frustrated life. "But what still horrifies me, is Jeremy's insanity. His hunger for money was more important than anything else—even human life." The last words came out in a rush of tears.

"Oh, my darling," Leon said, taking her gently into his arms. "You know," he began again after he saw, with the help of several little healing kisses, that Josina had recovered, "It used to make me smile when Jeremy treated me like such an inferior. All the time he was doing it, I could imagine his rage when I let it be known who I really was. I could just see his expression when he found out I was related to Martha Koster." He threw back his head and laughed. Then suddenly his expression changed and he snapped a small branch from a bush at the edge of the path.

"But I hated him for seducing Ida and then abandoning her. I wanted to beat him to within an inch of his life. But I kept telling myself that he was going to marry you, a young woman with nothing, which had to mean that he loved you a great deal. Besides, you said you were in love with him, and you were so vulnerable. I didn't want to hurt you, so I kept quiet. I just didn't feel I had any right to destroy your illusions...your happiness."

Finally, Josina was able to understand everything—Leon's words, his questions, the sarcastic way he had spoken of Jeremy and the struggle he had had not to give way to his true feelings.

"Do you remember," he asked in a playful tone of reproach, "how many times I asked you if you really loved him? Your answer was always the same. You always said you did."

Josina lowered her head in embarrassment. "I thought I did," she murmured. "I guess I just couldn't see him for what he really was. What I saw was what I wanted to see. He seemed to love me, and that was something I sorely needed. When I realized that I didn't love him, I felt trapped. I didn't know how to change things—how to tell everyone that I had made a big mistake."

"It's hard to know what love is," Leon said in a quiet voice, "until you really feel it. And then you know for sure. I loved you enough to want you to be happy, even if it meant that you could only be happy with another man. I loved you from the first minute I saw you." He paused, taking Josina in his strong arms, kissing her tenderly on her nose, her cheeks, her eyes. "Your beautiful face, your gray eyes and soft, sweet mouth." He lingered for a moment, Josina's heart racing, before he reached for her lips with his own. His kiss was gentle at first, and then insistent, passionate, drawing Josina into a vortex of feeling such as she had never experienced. They were one and the ecstasy of their touching was almost more than she could bear.

Faint, breathless, Josina drew away, afraid even to look into Leon's love-filled eyes.

"Josina, please look at me," Leon said huskily, tilting her face toward his. "I knew you were the woman I had been dreaming about, the woman I was sure could never exist."

Josina was trembling. She waited for a moment, hoping to control her voice. "It seems," she said in a voice that shook in spite of her efforts, "that we've both been struggling. I fought for a long time before I finally had to admit that I loved you."

Leon looked at Josina steadily, and the glow in his dark eyes warmed her. "You could love a modest game-keeper?" he asked with a playful smile.

"It is the man a woman loves, when her love is true."

Oh, how could she have ever hesitated? How could she have tried to deny the truth in her heart? Yes...from the very first time they had looked at each other, they had belonged together.

"When I realized I loved you, it was too late," Josina went on. "I had made a vow, and if I had not gone through with the marriage, I would have hurt the one person in the world who had been so incredibly kind to me. I couldn't risk hurting her, after she had taken me into her house and her heart. I didn't know, then, that she was my grandmother."

Josina couldn't help thinking that she had almost paid very dearly for her doubts and uncertainties.

"Our scruples very nearly lost us to each other," Leon said thoughtfully. "But somehow..." he mused, touching the talisman emerald in Josina's ring. "Somehow I think it would have all worked out for us no matter what."

Leon gazed into Josina's eyes tenderly, treasuring this woman whom he loved so completely. With his arms around her, his lips seeking hers, Josina knew that happiness was hers, was theirs. She surrendered herself to his embrace and passionately returned his kiss.

Don't miss these exciting Masquerades!

4. Lady in the Lion's Den by Elaine Reeve

The year is 1066. The place is England. A beautiful young Norman woman becomes a pawn in the struggle between Leowulf, a proud Saxon leader, and the conquering Normans.

5. Unwilling Betrothal by Christine James

Incredibly, Lady Annabelle Sarne finds herself virtually betrothed to three men–a French marquis, a rugged English army major and a mysterious stranger known only as André....

6. A Perfect Match by Julia Murray

The rigid rules of Regency England dictate that Miss Louisa Parke marry Lord Windlow–all because an innocent set of circumstances caused him to compromise her. Miss Parke is not at all pleased....

7. Frenchman's Harvest by Emma Gayle

Set in England and France in 1890, *Frenchman's Harvest* is an intriguing story of the romance between an orphaned English girl and the handsome son of her new French guardian.

8. Lysander's Lady by Patricia Ormsby

A delightful Regency romance in which an elegant young lady becomes the prize in a wager between a dangerous, unscrupulous marquis and a fashionable man-about-town.

9. Castle of the Mist by Valentina Luellen

The Scottish Highlands of the early eighteenth century are the setting for this thrilling tale in which a young widow must choose between the bond of blood and the bond of love.

MYSTIQUE BOOKS

Experience the warmth of love ... and the threat of danger!

MYSTIQUE BOOKS are a breathless blend of romance and suspense, passion and mystery. Let them take you on journeys to exotic lands—the sunny Caribbean, the enchantment of Paris, the sinister streets of Istanbul.

MYSTIQUE BOOKS

An unforgettable reading experience.
Now ... many previously published titles are once again available.
Choose from this great selection!

Don't miss any of these thrilling novels of love and adventure!

Choose from this list of exciting
MYSTIQUE BOOKS